GHOST DAYS

Geonn Cannon

Supposed Crimes LLC • Matthews, North Carolina

GHOST DAYS

CHAPTER ONE

1985

RED KITE, SASKATCHEWAN

The only colors in sight were the sickly brown of the prairie and the unsettling yellow of the sky. The two colors blurred together to obscure the flat horizon with an ochre-colored soup that upset the stomach. On top of being ugly, the day was the kind of hot that forced people outside to sit in its ugliness since it was impossible to just ignore it.

Erika Garza decided if she had to be outside anyway, she could at least get a little work done. Her plane needed an oil change and she didn't have any flights on the schedule, so now was as good a time as any. She flew a Cessna 402 with a white belly and a bright red stripe running along its center length. She'd bought it as a wreck, its life cut short by a bad fuel gauge and a rough landing in a field that had almost taken off a wing. She had nearly gone broke buying it even in that state, and the rest of her savings had gone into its resurrection. It was junk, it was almost twenty years old, and almost everything on it needed to be patched, repaired, or replaced before she even thought about taking it up in the air. So many of its vital parts had been replaced or swapped out that she wasn't sure the company would recognize it as one of their own. Its insides might have looked odd, but it got her where she needed to go and it was her pride and joy. She wanted to make sure its second life was long and fruitful.

Garza had the engine compartment open, her arms inside up to the elbows, when she heard the growl of an engine. She peeked around the cover and squinted down the road, perfectly framed by the Piper's propellers, and watched as a plume of dust became a car. She'd been working in just her undershirt, so she stepped off the stool and retrieved the shirt she'd draped over a strut on the wing. By the time she had it on and buttoned, suspenders pulled back up onto her shoulders, the car had turned off the main road and was fast approaching the small building that she proudly called an airport.

She wiped the grease her hands as she crossed the tarmac toward the now-idle vehicle. The driver's door opened and a scarecrow unfolded himself from behind the wheel. Tall, narrow everywhere but the shoulders, his clothes looking like they were filled with the bare minimum of a person, he took off his hat and tossed it onto the seat behind him. He looked toward the airport, pivoted his head toward Garza as she walked toward him, and made the decision to meet her halfway.

"Good afternoon, sir," the man shouted as he approached. "Might I have a moment of your time?"

Garza was glad he was still too far away to see her expression. "Ma'am, actually." It felt slightly wrong to be annoyed. She was dressed in men's clothing and, though she had a slight build, her hair was cut very short on the sides and shaggy on top. From a distance it would've been easy to make the mistake. Still, it rankled. She waited until she was a little closer before she continued. "Erika Garza. Owner, operator, pilot of Red Kite Aviation. How can I help you?"

He raised his eyebrows and leaned back slightly from her extended hand. She'd seen enough people who were put off or weirdly angry about discovering she was a woman that she could tell he was simply surprised. He finally extended his hand, offering an awkward but sincere smile as he gave her hand a weak squeeze and a simple up-down pump.

"Hello. My name is Saul P. Oakhill." His voice was clipped, every word enunciated perfectly, as if he was reciting them off a card hidden in his hand. "I am a banker, charged by a client to negotiate a difficult business deal in Calgary. It will require several weeks of travel to and from British Columbia and, rather than deal with commercial flights, I would~"

As he spoke, the passenger door of his car opened.

Where Saul had unfolded like a stick insect, the woman emerged like she had been poured out into the sun to expand to her full form. The wind immediately picked up her white dress and flapped it around her legs like a surrender. Erika was distracted by the long length of leg from ankle to knee, the passenger's hand coming down to prevent more than just a brief flash of thigh. The woman wore a man's hat pulled low over her eyes. It looked similar to the one Saul had removed when he got out of the car, and Erika questioned whether it was the same one. Her arms were bare, a smattering of freckles there darkened from too much time spent in the sun.

The passenger gave a panoramic look around the property and then, hands on her hips, walked over to join them. She wore driving goggles and a scarf that was tucked into the V of her dress so the tails wouldn't join her dress in waving in the wind.

Saul followed Garza's eyeline and saw the passenger approaching. His jaw tightened. "I thought you were staying in the car."

"It's hot as Hades in the blasted car," the woman said, her words colored by an unplaceable accent. She looked Garza up and down. "You're a woman."

"Not as much as you are," Garza said before she could stop the words.

The woman's expression didn't change, but her lips quirked slightly in a way that could have been a smile or a frown.

"Erika Garza," Saul said. "Christine Parrish."

"Pleasure," Parrish said.

Garza dipped her chin. "Sure," she said.

Saul cleared his throat. "So Miss Garza. Will you be able to handle that?"

"Hm? Oh." For a moment she'd misunderstood the question in a way that made her cheeks burn. It took her a second to realign her thoughts to remember what he'd said. "Yeah, I can handle that. Two trips per week?"

"Tuesday morning until Thursday, late afternoon," Saul confirmed. "You will deliver me to Calgary and return to bring me back. You will be given ample warning if the schedule should change for any reason."

Garza said, "Sure thing."

Her eyes were still on Parrish. She was looking at the plane, hopefully admiring it, possibly trying to gauge if it was capable of what they were asking it to do. There were tiny diamonds of sweat on her throat, making her shine. Saul had obviously noticed her distraction but seemed unwilling to speak up about it. Garza decided to acknowledge the staring in what she hoped would also work to gather information about the odd couple.

"Why don't we work out the details in the office? I've got a couple of fans, and your wife can get something cold to drink."

Parrish looked away from the plane so sharply it looked like she'd been slapped. "I'm not his wife," she said in the time it took Saul to get out "We're~" He pressed his lips together and swallowed the rest of what he'd been about to say.

"Your acquaintance." Garza gestured toward the office.

Saul led the way, followed by Garza. She glanced back to see Parrish had remained where she was standing, eyes tracking Garza, face still completely unreadable, then fell into line behind them. Garza faced forward again to see Saul, with his rigid and unwavering gait, had gained a lead. She moved a little faster to catch up, certain that if she turned to look, she would see Parrish moving along in their wake in no hurry at all. In the few seconds they'd spent together, Garza had figured out that Christine Parrish was a woman who moved through the world at her own speed.

Despite two fans - one high and one low - and all the windows being open, the office was still sweltering. Saul took one of the seats behind the desk while Garza shuffled past the piles of papers and the filing cabinet to get to her own chair.

Parrish entered after they had both sat down, and she took off the hat so she could fan her face with it. Curly chin-length hair fell free, perfectly parted to frame her face. At first glance she looked blonde, but Garza realized on second glance that it was actually as white as her dress. Not gray, not silver, not even platinum blonde, but white. It was a striking look, and it almost made her forget Saul was also in the room. She had to force her eyes down onto the papers, which she began shuffling to find the standard long-term hire contract.

"Okay, um, most of this is going to be boilerplate, but we can go over it if you like. Pricewise and whatnot."

"Price won't be an issue."

"Must be nice."

Parrish wandered to the far side of the room. She lifted off the driving goggles so she could see the maps on the wall more clearly. Garza wished she was closer and turned the other way so she could get a look at her eyes. She could ask her to have a seat next to Saul, but she didn't want to draw any more attention to her fascination than she already had.

"And if there are any fees you'd like me to explain…"

"I'm well-traveled, Miss Garza. I assure you, I know how this works."

She was glad she had the pitch down so well that she could recite it without thinking. The words fell out of her mouth while her brain was focused on Parrish, who had leaned forward to examine a map of the province. Her left hand was still using the hat to waft air toward her face, but she was shining with sweat regardless.

"The flight will be just over two hours."

"That will be fine," Saul said. "Would you prefer full payment upfront?"

"We'll do a case-by-case basis, depending on weather conditions and if the plane needs maintenance. I'd rather not get money than have to pay it back."

His face changed so that it almost looked like a smile. "I can agree with that logic, Miss Garza. I believe we have an agreement."

"Just sign here," she said, passing a pen to him.

Parrish moved away from the maps. The woman didn't seem to walk when she moved; she drifted. Her feet barely made any sound on the floor as she walked, stepping quietly until she was directly behind Saul's chair. She watched him sign, then looked up at Garza.

"Do you allow passengers?"

"Uh."

Parrish nodded to the window. "Seats six, by my counting. Surely it wouldn't hurt if I tagged along to see him off and then you brought me back."

Garza said, "Uh. The, um, weight of three passengers requires more fuel than if it's just two, so it would affect the price. I'm not sure it would be worth it to just tag along to say goodbye."

"Mm, I suppose not." She smoothed her hand over the top of Saul's head, stroking him like he was a pet cat. He shifted his eyes as if trying to look behind himself without turning his head. "Worth asking, though."

"I guess so." Garza cleared her throat and stood up. "So. Uh, first flight will be next Tuesday at nine-thirty in the morning. Calgary is an hour behind, so that gets you there by lunchtime. Return flight on Thursday, I'll be at the airport at five-thirty pm, local time, to bring you home."

Saul stood and extended his hand across the desk. "I look forward to flying with you, Miss Garza. Tuesday at nine-thirty."

She shook his hand. "I'll see you then."

Parrish replaced the fedora on her head as she stepped out of his way. Saul led the way out of the office, Parrish falling into step behind him. It should have looked subservient, but to Garza it seemed more like he was escorting her back out into the sun. Garza followed them as far as the door, stopping at the threshold to watch them walk to their car. Parrish had moved to Saul's side and slipped her arm around his. The sun was hitting her at just the right angle for the shape of her body to be highlighted against her dress. White dress. White hair.

Saul and his "acquaintance" got into the car. Garza waited until the engine came to life and they had started rolling before she went back into the office. She still needed to finish working on the engine, but first she needed the coldest drink she could scrounge up. She was glad she'd come up with the fuel excuse to keep the woman from riding along for the drop-offs and pickups.

She didn't trust herself to spend two hours alone in the plane with that woman.

Chapter Two

Tuesday

The first trip to Calgary was as uneventful as Garza hoped and feared. Two hours in the plane sitting next to a man who might as well have been a mannequin. He greeted her in the office and followed her to the plane, a silent shadow. He paid close attention when she gave her safety briefing despite claiming to be well-traveled. Then he folded his hands in his lap and faced forward through takeoff. She never saw him lean toward the windows to appreciate the view, never saw him white-knuckle his briefcase to indicate anxiety, and he never once shifted to a more comfortable position.

When they landed, he thanked her, gave her a firm handshake, and confirmed he would be back Thursday at five-thirty. Then he turned and walked away.

Garza fueled up the plane, got some lunch, and turned around for the trip home. Flying back alone was only marginally different than flying with Saul. The main change was that the silence was much less awkward.

When she landed, her only thoughts were of taking a bath to wash off the flight and maybe taking a nap until the day started cooling off. She was so distracted by the fantasy that she almost missed the card stuck between the office door and the frame. She pulled it free, looked around as if whoever left it was lurking around, and read the message scrawled on the front.

MEET ME AT THE REACH, 7:30PM - CP

She frowned, thumped the card with her finger, and slipped it into the pocket of her trousers. CP was obviously Christine Parrish. The Reach was a bar in Red Kite, the closest town to the airport and probably where the Oakhills - rather, Mr. Oakhill and his companion - lived. It was just under two miles away and Garza only had her motorcycle. She had no intention of riding that far after she had spent four hours aboard a plane. She tossed the card onto her desk as she passed through her office, already forgotten.

Beyond the office, she'd converted the rest of the building into her living space. A large living room, smallish bathroom, cramped bedroom, and a kitchen that barely allowed space for both an icebox and a stove. It was plenty for her, and she kept it tidy to give the impression of having more room than she actually had.

The flight had eaten up her whole morning and the first chunk of the afternoon, prompting her brain to consider the entire day finished. She did take a bath and then a nap, but woke up with only enough motivation to work on her books. She added Saul's flight to her logs and spent the next few hours working on her budget for the coming month.

She got so lost in the numbers that she didn't realize how late it had gotten until a pair of headlights swept across the front of the building. The airport was far enough away from anything else that no one could have pulled in by accident, so she lifted her head to see if maybe it was a last-minute customer.

It was too dark to tell much about the car, even if she could've identified one kind from another, but somehow, even before she got out of the car, Garza knew it would be Parrish.

Tonight she wore a scoop-neck white shirt that clung to her curves, tight enough to look painted on tucked into a pair of equally snug blue jeans. Garza put down her pen and leaned back in her chair, tracking the visitor through the window.

When she knocked, Garza said, "C'min."

Parrish entered. She kept the door open, hand on the knob, hip cocked. She raised an eyebrow.

"You didn't show up."

Garza looked at the clock to see it was almost eight. She shrugged. "I didn't feel like drinking. Or riding my bike home drunk, after dark. Sorry. I probably should've called."

"I don't like being stood up." Parrish closed the door and walked to the chair Saul had used on the first visit. She placed her hands on the backrest like she planned to give it a shoulder massage. "Did you deliver my lovely man safe and sound?"

Garza nodded, waggling the pen between two fingers just to be doing something besides just sitting there under this woman's gaze. "The trip went as planned, mm-hmm." She watched Parrish very carefully, trying to figure out what the woman's game was. "What's that accent? I can't quite place it."

"Australia," Parrish said, smiling widely, as if just saying the country's name gave her inordinate pride. "Good ear."

She stepped around the chair and sat down, crossing her legs. Something about the way she sat - slightly slumped, hands lazily draped over the arms, one leg crossed over the opposite knee - made her look like an idle king entertaining a jester. Parrish stared at her so hard that, after just a few seconds, Garza started to squirm uncomfortably.

"You're probably wondering about me and Saul. Our relationship."

"I don't pry into my clients' personal lives," Garza said.

Parrish smiled. "A lot of people wonder about it. I've been called Mrs. Oakhill more times than I care to count. But I have no interest in anything official, and he doesn't care that we aren't married. It keeps things manageable. It keeps things interesting. You've met him. Does he strike you as an *exciting* person to spend your life with? Or did you want to jump out of the damn plane after an hour alone with him?"

Garza twisted her mouth to avoid answering. "So you don't love him."

"I didn't say that. I have very deep feelings for him. I desperately wanted him for a very long time before we finally got together. And... hm." She laughed at a memory, her eyes focused on a spot somewhere above Garza's head. "He wanted me just as badly when we first got together. All that pent-up energy and desire... It was electric. For a while. But then things calmed down. He was the dog who caught the car and didn't have the first idea what to do afterward.

"So we had a long talk, and we decided the best choice was to ignore the ordinary thing, the normal way of life, and just do what makes sense for us. To make *ourselves* happy instead of trapping ourselves in a box. Do you know what he'll be doing in Calgary when he's not working?"

Garza shrugged.

Parrish put a hand next to her mouth, pretending to share a secret. "He's looking for a man to take to bed. He likes to be on the bottom, receiving. He also likes to use his mouth."

"Oh." Garza's discomfort skyrocketed. She cleared her throat and, for lack of anything more clever, said again, "Oh. And you're fine with this?"

Parrish laughed softly, huskily. "You think I'm going to let him have all the fun? I find ways to keep myself busy when he's on these business trips."

Garza could feel her heart beating in her throat. "I suppose that makes sense."

"Heh. Sometimes we do have sex, just like ordinary folk. I don't mind it. He's good at it, and he tends to focus a lot on me. It can be therapeutic. Stress relief. Like exercise. Almost mechanical, sometimes. Nothing to write home about but it gets the job done. Gets me where I need to go, if you know what I'm saying."

"I know."

"I'm sure you do," Parrish said under her breath.

She leaned forward and crossed her arms on the front edge of Garza's desk. The low collar of her shirt gaped just enough to show a hint of her cleavage, where droplets of sweat were highlighted by the desk lamp. She bit her bottom lip as she scanned Garza's face.

"But sometimes I need more. It's been a long time since I've gotten more. And I'm feeling the need. It's like a burning inside me, and I know if I don't take care of it soon, it's gonna burn up all my insides. So that's why I came to you, Miss Garza. Erika. You can give me what I want."

Garza forced herself to meet Parrish's unwavering gaze. "And what would that be?"

"I want you to fuck me like an animal."

It wasn't a request or an invitation. It was permission.

Garza stood and came around the desk at a speed that made Parrish brace for collision, but she was still knocked back a few steps when Garza slammed into her. She cupped Parrish's face and kissed her hard. All the anxieties and stolen looks and the thoughts she'd hated herself for having faded away, suddenly okay because Parrish had crossed the line first. Parrish's hands ended up on Garza's hips, curling in the beltloops of her pants, holding on as Garza walked her to the wall and pinned her there.

"Say you want me," Parrish gasped against Garza's mouth. "I saw the way you were looking at me. Say the words."

"I want you," Garza said, going back for another kiss.

Then suddenly Parrish pushed her away, so violently that it was almost enough to break through the fog of arousal. "What..."

"Beg." Parrish rolled her hips forward suggestively, resting one hand on the waistband of her jeans as she ran the other up her stomach to her breasts, untucking the shirt in the process. "Beg for me."

Garza licked her lips, tasting Parrish's lipstick. "Please," Garza said.

Parrish's hand disappeared under her shirt. "Is that really how you beg, Erika?"

Garza held eye contact as she slowly knelt down. "Please, Christine. I want you. I've wanted you from the moment I saw you." She wouldn't drop onto her hands to crawl, not unless the rules of the game dictated it, but she walked forward on her knees until she could put her hands on Parrish's hips. She pushed her palms up until she felt skin. She leaned down to kiss the exposed stretch of belly, parting her lips to explore with her tongue, sliding higher. Parrish lifted her shirt a bit at a time to give her more runway to work with.

"Please," Erika spoke with her lips against the warm skin. "Can I have you, Christine?"

The hair on the back of Garza's head wasn't long, but Parrish still managed to find enough to grab a handful and tilt her head back to look up at her.

"No."

She bucked her hips forward, bumping Garza just enough to knock her on her ass. Anger flared in Garza's brain as she lay on the floor. She bared her teeth to throw the cruel, teasing bitch out of her office, but Parrish didn't give her a chance to speak.

"You can't *have* me," she said flatly. "If you *want* me you have to take me."

Garza let the words, and their meaning, sink in. She put her hands on the floor and pushed herself up. Parrish's eyes never left her as she rose to her feet. The white-blonde seductress remained against the wall, her shirt still lifted to just below her breasts. The hand she'd used to push Garza away hovered near the button of her pants. Garza slowly got back to her feet. She was shaking, both from desire and irritation at being played like this. But she had to admit, while it wasn't a game she would've chosen, she was finding it...

...intriguing.

"You want me to take you?"

Parrish's eyes flashed. She lifted her chin. "If you think you can."

Garza let the silence hang between them. "Get out of here."

The arousal and playfulness fled from Parrish's face. She let her shirt drop and stood up straighter. "What?"

"You heard me. Get the fuck out of my office."

"I-I'm sorry. I thought~"

"I don't care. Go."

Parrish smoothed down her shirt, then ran a hand through her hair. All the fire had gone out of her eyes and she looked abashed and awkward now. All trace of verve and control was gone as if it had never been there.

"I-I'm sorry if I went too far too fast. It's just~"

"I didn't ask for an explanation."

"Right."

Parrish brushed past Garza, shoulders slightly hunched, head down in shame. Garza watched her go, waiting until her hand was on the doorknob before she moved.

Garza rushed Parrish, molded her body to Parrish's back as she pressed her hard against the door. Parrish placed her hands flat against the door and looked back over her shoulder with a surprised gasp. Parrish was taller than her, so Garza had to lift her heels off the ground to line up their faces properly. The white blonde curls fell across her face but Garza could still see the eye, wide and startled, through the veil. She had one hand on Parrish's shoulder and angled her hips away, then dropped her other hand. She cupped Parrish's ass through her blue jeans, hard, and then pulled back to give her a hard swat.

Parrish's entire body tensed. She let out a high-pitched yelp of surprise, followed by a shudder that went from her shoulders all the way down to her legs. She placed her hands flat against the wall to brace herself. She arched her back, tacitly giving Garza permission to keep going. So Garza spanked her again, and this time Parrish's reaction was a moan, teeth digging into a crimson bottom lip. Her eyes drifted closed.

"No. You look at me."

Parrish's eyes opened, locked on her.

"I don't like playing games, Miss Parrish."

"I'm sorry."

"You better be. But if you need to hear it..." She brushed the hair away from Parrish's ear and leaned in close to whisper. "I want you. I've been thinking about you since the moment you got out of that car, and if you tell me I can rip off your clothes and do anything that comes to mind, I'm going to do that. So say it."

Parrish was shaking so much, their bodies pressed so tightly together, that Garza could feel it through her whole body.

"Take me," Parrish said. "Do whatever you want to me."

Garza spun her around and kissed her. Parrish's teeth scraped Garza's bottom lip just enough to hurt. Garza took both of Parrish's hands, lifted her arms up, pinned them against the wall over her head. She spread her fingers so she could hold the crossed wrists with one hand and lower the other, finally running her fingers along all those lovely curves. She explored the small but perfect breasts, seemingly sized to her palm specifically. She traced the smooth line from Parrish's underarm to the slight flare out of her hip. She had to use her weak hand to get the button and fly open, but she managed it without breaking the kiss or releasing Parrish's hands.

"You're so fucking beautiful," Garza said before kissing her again. Parrish melted against her with a moan that shot down to the base of Garza's spine. "Tell me I can have you all night."

"I'm yours until Thursday," Parrish said. "All yours."

Garza pulled her away from the wall. She let one of Parrish's arms go but kept her grip on the other, walking backward.

"Where are we going?"

"Bedroom," Garza said.

Parrish smiled and pushed her hair out of her face. All trace of tease and superiority had faded from her expression, and all Garza could see now was excitement. She relaxed her fingers and slid them down, taking Parrish's hand in hers so it was more of a caress than a leading gesture.

She had no idea what was about to happen. She was terrified and thrilled in equal measure. But she knew whatever happened, Christine Parrish was a willing participant, and right now that was all she needed to know. She focused on Parrish's icy blue eyes until the dark hallway made it impossible to see her features, and they vanished into the darkness of her house together.

CHAPTER THREE

Wednesday

Garza woke sore the next morning. She was naked, and parts of her were still wet. She brushed her hand through the wetness on her thigh and tapped her finger against her tongue, trying to figure out what it was and if it was hers or Parrish's. The results were inconclusive, but she thought it was most likely sweat because her bedroom was already ridiculously hot.

She got out of bed, feet briefly tangled around the sheets, and went to the window she'd neglected to open the night before due to her guest. The frame creaked and squealed as she muscled it up, not caring that she was naked and on display. This far from town, there was no one to see her except moose or a deer, and they were welcome to a show if they wanted one.

With a meager breeze now blowing through the bedroom, she turned to face the empty bed. She hadn't heard Parrish leave, but she wasn't surprised to find herself alone.

Last night had been a frenzy. Parrish had said she wanted to be fucked like an animal. Garza would have bet cash money she never would have been capable of that, but somehow she'd managed. She swore she'd heard ripping when she took off Parrish's clothes. Had she actually *ripped* the clothes off a woman...? Every gasp or cry of pleasure or excitement from Parrish had spurred her on, made her more crazed, made her want to do something crazier to top whatever had earned that noise.

Regrettably, she remembered very little of the specific moments. Lots of kissing. A soft and somehow cool hand reaching up under her shirt to blindly explore. Then skin to skin, sweat sticking them together in unusual places. Gentle fingers teasing her nipples, pinching and twisting before exploring lower. Stretching her body on top of Parrish so that her hip was between Parrish's legs, using her feet to thrust herself upward, rubbing herself against Parrish, who had her legs wrapped around Garza and lifted her hips to meet each thrust.

There was spanking, biting, Parrish's hair was pulled. They swore at each other, about each other, in praise and frustration.

"Tell me you want me," Parrish whispered against Garza's cheek, three of her fingers inside Garza up to the knuckle. "Use my name. Please."

"I want you, Christine Parrish," Garza whispered.

She remembered how Parrish's breath had hitched, almost like she was crying, but then her orgasm briefly blacked her out so she couldn't confirm tears. She didn't know when they'd finally fallen asleep. As exhausted as she'd been, Parrish wouldn't have needed to use stealth to sneak out undetected.

Garza left the bedroom mostly naked, the heat so oppressive that she only bothered with a pair of briefs. She second-guessed that decision when she reached the kitchen and found Parrish sitting at the breakfast table reading the newspaper. Garza's robe was just a little too small on her, riding high on the leg and just snug enough on the chest that she couldn't cinch it closed. This left the majority of her leg and a thin strip of bare skin down the center of her chest was exposed. Not that Garza, on full display had any room to judge her level of nudity.

Parrish lowered the paper and ran her eyes down Garza's body. "Good morning."

There was a mug on the table in front of her. "You made coffee?"

"God no." Parrish lifted the mug and tilted it slightly so Garza could see the contents. "This is just OJ. You can drink coffee on a day like this?"

"Not if I have exactly one cup of orange juice left."

Parrish looked sheepish. "Sorry."

"Don't worry about it. I like water just fine."

She took a glass from the cupboard and filled it from the tap. The pipes had made the water tepid, and she grimaced as she took a sip and walked to sit across from Parrish. She was self-conscious about being next to naked, but going back to the bedroom felt like a retreat. Parrish put down the newspaper and pushed the mug to the center of the table.

"We can share."

Garza wrinkled her nose. "You've already drunk from that."

Parrish grinned devilishly. "Now you're worried about germs, sweetheart? After the places you put your tongue last night?"

Garza blushed. She hated that she blushed, but she couldn't stop herself. She'd had Parrish's toes in her mouth. Sharing a mug of juice couldn't be any less hygienic than that. She nodded her thanks, picked up the mug, and took a drink.

"You look even better in daylight," Parrish said.

"You're not so bad yourself."

"Do you have any work you need to do today?"

Garza shook her head. "No flights until tomorrow when I go get your boy. Why, what did you have in mind?"

"I could make up for stealing your juice by taking you out to breakfast."

"In town?" Garza stiffened slightly. "You sure that's such a good idea?"

Parrish smirked, the predator gleam returning to her eyes. "Why? Worried I won't be able to control my desires? Or worried about yourself?"

Her foot slid up the inside of Garza's calf.

"Worried about how it might look. Saul out of town, you—"

"Having breakfast with my new friend?"

Garza moved her leg away from the rising foot. "I'm not the kind of person who hangs out in town with friends. Trust me, people would find it weird."

Parrish shrugged. "Well, I don't know about you, but I have to eat something soon. You don't have anything here."

"I have plenty here," Garza said, looking at the kitchen cabinets as if she could inventory the contents through the doors. She looked back at Parrish and tried to read her face. "So. Is that what we are? Friends? After last night?"

"Oh, hurrah, *that* conversation."

She reached for a pack of cigarettes that Garza hadn't seen. She tapped one out, pinched it between her lips. She got up and went to the kitchen.

"Skinny drawer by the sink," Garza said.

Parrish found the matches and used one to light the cigarette. She took a drag and blew the smoke toward the ceiling as she walked back to the table. She rested her shoulder against the fridge. Her robe fell open, exposing her naked lower body. The hair between her legs was slightly darker than her head, but it was close enough to make Garza believed her peculiar color was natural rather than bleached.

"I don't see why we have to give it a name," Parrish said.

"You don't much like labeling things, do you?" Garza asked. "You and Saul aren't married, aren't a couple, you're just... together."

"Keeps things easy," Parrish said. "It allows wonderful things like last night to happen without headaches or heartbreaks. And we don't have to worry about sharing our life stories, or if we're compatible outside the bedroom, or any of that nonsense. We can focus on the fucking, which we've already discovered we're very, very good at. Isn't that better? And isn't it better than boxing yourself in with some stupid title like 'girlfriend' and 'boyfriend'? Ugh." She wrinkled her nose and took another drag. "It sounds so juvenile, anyway. Like we're teenagers going steady."

Garza stood up. She went to Parrish and pulled the two sides of the robe together, then tied the belt in a secure loop. Parrish watched her do that with an amused smile.

"Some of us like to know where we stand, Miss Parrish."

Parrish used a deft twist of her fingers to turn the cigarette around. She held it in front of Garza, who waited two beats before she put her lips around it and breathed in. The smoke burned her throat, but she refused to cough and didn't exhale until she absolutely couldn't stand it anymore. She was aware that her lips were touching something Parrish's lips had just touched, and somehow that intimacy seemed deeper than just kissing.

Abandoning the cigarette, Parrish stepped closer and hooked her thumbs under the elastic of Garza's briefs.

"And for some of us," Parrish said, "where we stand is not as important as where we kneel."

She sank to her knees, pulling the underwear down Garza's legs with the same motion. She let the cotton fall to pool around her bare feet, then put her hands on Garza's ass to pull her forward.

Garza closed her eyes, pinching the cigarette with one hand as she braced herself against the fridge with the other. She closed her eyes and let out a long slow breath of smoke as Parrish's tongue touched her. She relaxed. She eased her legs apart, angling her lower body so Parrish didn't have to push her tongue out quite as far.

Kneeling, she decided, was good.

Maybe not in the long run. Definitely not forever. But right now, in this kitchen, she could say without hesitation that kneeling was very good.

They faced each other in the bathtub that night. The bathroom light was off to keep the room cooler, but the bedroom light shined through the open door and let them see each other. Garza had originally drawn the bath to wash away the sweat from the day. When she finished that task, she turned and saw Parrish standing naked in the doorway. Who could turn down a request like that?

Parrish's legs were on the outside, knees breaking the surface. Garza had positioned her shorter legs in the center of the tub. Their four knees looked like a shining archipelago separating the continents of their bodies. Garza reclined against the curve of the tub, her arms resting on the edge. Parrish's arms were inside the tub pushing her breasts together, intentionally or not, and Garza found herself staring at the pale pink nipples she'd spent the past few hours getting to know very well. Parrish's face, throat, and arms were dotted with freckles of varying darkness. The parts of her that were usually exposed - arms, hands, face, were obviously darker. But more clusters were scattered across her breasts, stomach, thighs... Garza hoped she would have time to map them all.

They hadn't had a real conversation since that morning. Parrish had made her come with her mouth, and then Garza fucked her on the floor of the kitchen. Then they dressed and Parrish drove them to town to buy groceries, since Garza finally had to admit she really didn't have much food in the house. She was self-conscious as she walked the aisles of the store, certain everyone could smell what they'd done. She thought Parrish felt the same way, the way she hid behind Garza's shoulder and refused to wander out of her sight. It was like she didn't want anyone else to get too close to her. They'd washed up, to a degree, in the sink before they left the house, but she knew that was a piss-poor substitute to actual bathing.

When they got back to the house, Parrish offered to make them a meal. "It's my one concession to domesticity," she explained, "and I only do it because I love cooking." They sat down together to eat, and Garza tried to picture being okay with just this. No deeper feelings, no intimate conversations, just wild and passionate sex and quiet meals together. It wouldn't be the worst thing in the world. And the sex *was* phenomenal. They'd fucked again after lunch, napped, and now they were in the bath together.

"I know you said we weren't going to have deeper conversations," Garza said, "but I've gotta know how you usually fill your days. Do you have chores or a job or something? You just spent the entire day lounging around my house naked. Why's your schedule so free?"

"I don't have any responsibilities that can't be put off for a day or two." Parrish grinned and closed her eyes, settling back against the tub. "Mr. Oakhill makes a very good living."

"So you're a kept woman?"

"You say that like it's a bad thing."

Garza said, "So you get a place to stay. Spending money, probably. And what exactly does Saul get from you?"

Parrish raised an eyebrow. "You've been appreciating it too much to have already forgotten how good it is."

"I thought this whole endeavor was because *he* didn't appreciate... that."

"He appreciates it," Parrish said unconvincingly. "He definitely doesn't mind it. He gets hard just like any other man, barely takes any prompting from me to get him ready to go. But I guess if you want a more sincere answer, I give him respectability. I give him, mm... normal. His bank has parties. His colleagues invite him to barbecues with the big boss. A man of a certain age showing up unchaperoned? Well, that would raise eyebrows. So I pretty myself up and put my arm around his, we kiss in his boss' backyard so he'll be remembered at promotion time."

Garza shook her head. "I couldn't live like that."

"Like what?"

"A prop."

Parrish rolled her eyes. "We all do what we have to in this life. This is far less demeaning than some other things I could be doing to make a living."

Garza grunted. She had a point there.

She shifted against the tub, trying to sit up straighter, and her foot slipped forward and brushed firmly between Parrish's legs. Parrish jumped, chuckled, and then settled back into place.

"Well, hi there," she said.

Garza considered her options. Then she moved her foot again, this time intentionally resting it against Parrish's sex. She pressed down just hard enough to make herself known. Parrish tensed, lowered her chin, locked her eyes on Garza.

"What are you doing?" Parrish asked under her breath.

"Not sure," Garza admitted. "This, I think..."

She bent her knee a little, moving the arch of her foot until she felt Parrish's softness against the meaty part of her foot just under her big toe. She rolled her ankle like she was crushing a cigarette in slow motion. Just the slightest amount of pressure, a smooth roll. Parrish lifted her arms out of the water and gripped the edge of the tub with both hands, rolling her head back until her chin pointed to the ceiling. She was breathing hard now, and Garza watched the rise and fall of her breasts as she moved her foot in a way that felt alien but also strangely familiar.

Parrish moved her hand under the water and loosely gripped Garza's ankle, meaning to guide her, but Garza shook her head.

"Don't. Let me."

Parrish put her hand back on the edge of the tub, closed her eyes. "I can't believe how amazing it feels. Weird... but..." She sighed and rolled her head back. "Amazing."

Garza didn't know if she'd go as far as amazing, but it was certainly interesting. And it let her watch Parrish's pleasure from a distance, which she greatly enjoyed. Her foot wasn't as limber as a hand, and her leg moved more awkwardly than an arm for this purpose, but when she figured out the angle and the pressure, Parrish arched her back and closed her legs around her calf.

"There, don't stop. Oh God..."

Garza watched Parrish's face as she came, her jaw trembling, eyelids fluttering. When her body relaxed, and reached down and pulled Garza's foot up out of the water and placed it on her stomach, stroking it with her fingers in a gentle massage. She sat up straighter, opened her eyes, and after a few seconds focused them on Garza.

"You just gave me an orgasm with your foot, Miss Garza."

"Yeah," Garza said. "Didn't know I could do that."

Parrish let go of her foot and pushed herself up. Garza was mesmerized by the water cascading down her curves, dripping from her nipples and down her thighs. She stood above Garza for a moment, the birth of Venus all over again, and then she stepped out of the water and stood dripping on the mat. She held out her hand to Garza.

"Let's see what some other parts of your body can do."

CHAPTER FOUR

Thursday

"You dress like a man."

Garza rolled over, put her hands behind her head, and stretched her legs out from under the blanket. She'd been awake for a few minutes, stirred by Parrish sliding out from under her to go to the bathroom, but she hadn't opened her eyes or shifted position. She had almost fallen back to sleep when Parrish ruined it by speaking, forcing her to see why the other woman hadn't come back to bed. She was standing in front of the closet, fully nude, examining the shirts hanging in order of color. There wasn't much variety, but Garza could see the shift from dark white to brown even if no one else could.

"I dress comfortably," Garza argued. "It's not my fault that they market those things to men."

"So you're not playing dress-up?" She found a pair of trousers and stepped into them, tugging them up to her hips. Parrish was taller and Garza was wider at the hips, but she was able to get them buttoned. "Not trying to be a man or trick people?"

"Well," Garza said, enjoying the show, "it helps if they don't realize I'm a woman until they're actually standing in front of me. Harder for them to suddenly decide to go with someone else. I don't have any desire to be a man, but letting people assume I am one certainly has its benefits."

"I thought you were a man at first," Parrish admitted. "It was the main reason I got out of the car. I wanted to get a closer look at you."

Garza raised an eyebrow. "So you planned this from the start?"

"Well, not *this* exactly." She slipped on one of Garza's shirts. The sleeves were too short, so she rolled them up to her elbows. "But a strapping young mechanic-slash-pilot was a prospect I couldn't pass up. When I saw you were a woman, *well...* I spent the whole drive home thinking of the possibilities."

She found a fedora on the top shelf of the closet and put it on, tucking her hair up underneath. She left the shirt unbuttoned so that when she turned around and spread her arms out, her breasts and stomach were on full display. She grinned and then put her hands on her hips.

"What do you think?" She ran her finger along the brim of the hat. "Do I make a good boy?"

"You're lacking a few parts," Garza said, "but I'm not going to miss 'em."

Parrish put her hands in her pockets and slumped her shoulders a bit, adding a swagger to her walk as she paced in front of the bed.

"Maybe if I dressed like this all the time, Saul would be a little more excitable."

Garza felt a twinge of jealousy at the mention of him, but she fought it down. She knew exactly what this was, and she couldn't deny the tingles building from the sight of Parrish dressed like a man.

"Maybe you could borrow that get-up. Give him a real welcome home." She thrust suggestively with her hips.

"It would be a little hard to explain where they came from."

Garza furrowed her brow. "Just tell him they're mine."

Parrish laughed. She climbed onto the bed and straddled Garza's legs, walking up her body until she could settle on her waist.

"Then he'd wonder why I'm borrowing clothes from you."

Garza propped herself up onto her elbows. "You're not going to tell him about us?"

Parrish looked horrified at the thought. "Why in the world would I do that?"

"You said he knew... you both had a... an arrangement."

"We do. But I don't give him details. And I certainly don't want to know what he's getting up to in Calgary. These are ghost days, you understand? They're not normal days that add up on the calendar. They're the special days. Like your birthday or Christmas or the first day of summer vacation. The last day of summer vacation. The most special of days, when it feels like anything can happen. Because anything *can* happen."

"Ghost days," Garza said quietly.

"And no one else gets to be part of our ghost days." She put her hand in the center of Garza's chest and gently urged her down onto her back. When she was flat again, Parrish moved her hand to caress Garza's breast. She pinched the nipple between her first two fingers. "The stuff happening in Calgary is all for him. And this is all for us. Is that okay?"

Garza tried not to be distracted by her nipples getting hard under Parrish's touch, or by how good Parrish looked in her clothes, or how great it was being under her.

"Do you know how weird it's going to be sitting in a plane with him for two hours and not saying anything?"

"You think it will be *less* weird if he knows we've spent the past couple days fucking?"

She had a point there. "So I'm just choosing between which flavor of awkwardness I'm more comfortable with."

Parrish stopped playing with her nipple and started idly running her hands over Garza's chest. Her fingers were splayed to cover as much space as possible.

"And this keeps things between us. We don't have to worry about how *he* would feel about being in a plane with *you*. Ignorance is bliss, after all. As long as I'm happy, he doesn't need to know who is making me happy."

"I guess," Garza said.

Parrish bit her bottom lip. "What time do you have to be in the air?"

"I'm picking him up at 5:30. I want to be there and refueled when he's ready to go, so I should probably leave here by two."

Parrish looked at the clock, nodded, and bent down to kiss Garza.

"Plenty of time."

Garza saw Mr. Oakhill's car on the road below the plane as she took off. Parrish stuck her arm out the window and waved, so Garza wagged the wings a bit in response. She still didn't know how she felt about their agreement. Keeping quiet felt illicit, like cheating, because that's exactly what it was without Saul's side of the story. But she couldn't exactly ask him to confirm without giving everything away. The man was logical, he would know there's only one reason she would ask about that. So she had to take Parrish's word that it was true and hope for the best.

However she felt about the situation long-term, she was grateful there was a solid endpoint to it for now. She could put some literal and figurative distance between herself and Christine Parrish so she could get her head on straight and think clearly about what to do next.

It was so risky to mix business with literal pleasure. She never fucked a client (*"Hah!"*) and she didn't see how fucking a client's wife was anything but a lateral move.

The 'hah' had been so real to her that she actually looked over her shoulder to make sure she was really alone in the plane. No sign of anyone, let alone the person she knew the voice had belonged to, so she faced forward and ignored it. She had two hours to get her thoughts in order before she would have to sit next to the man she was potentially cuckolding.

"Not that it bothered you before."

Garza bent her head to the left, the right, keeping her eyes straight ahead, not daring to look in the copilot's seat. If she just ignored the voice in her head, it would fade. It would stop getting in the way.

Lips warm against her ear, she shuddered. "Just a bit of fun," Renee Barrett whispered, her fingers unbuttoning Garza's shirt. They were only a few feet away from the rest of the class. She could hear their voices, the music, celebrating their graduation. She remembered the weight of Renee's body pinning her to the outside wall of the hangar. Not that Garza was doing anything to escape. She kept perfectly still, like she was trying to become invisible, to sink into the metal of the wall, if that was the only way to escape Renee's touch and ignore how much she wanted it.

"Mrs. Barrett..." Garza said.

"Mm-mm. Not here, not now," Renee said, placing a kiss on her jaw, "we're just two people. Erika... and..."

"Renee." Her voice was a harsh whisper.

"Good girl." Renee's voice was a soft purr. "Two people who deserve a little relaxation. It's no different than touching yourself in the shower. Or under the covers when you go to bed. Which do you prefer, Erika? Do you touch yourself in the shower or in bed?"

Garza's cheeks burned, both in the memory and reliving it on the plane. The question was a trap, no option for saying she didn't do it at all, no opportunity to lie. Her mouth was bone dry, as if all the moisture in her body was going somewhere else. She squirmed and finally looked Renee in the eye. Her instructor, more than a decade her senior, but *for fuck's sake* why did that make it hotter?

"In bed," Garza finally admitted.

Renee smiled, which drew Garza's attention to her lips. "I like doing it in bed, too. I like feeling the sheets on my bare legs."

Garza had responded to that information with a guttural whimper, a noise she didn't know she could make.

"We could watch each other do it sometime," Renee suggested. At some point, her hand had moved into Garza's now fully-unbuttoned shirt, and her fingertips were hot on her collarbone. "Would you like that, Erika?"

"Yes, ma'am."

"Good."

Renee leaned in and pressed her lips to the corner of Garza's mouth, then kissed her hard and passionate. Garza cried out, the sound muffled by Renee's tongue, but then she leaned into it. She clung to Renee, desperate to make her first kiss last as long as possible before it ended. She'd fought this for so long, denied this attraction, ignored the images that popped into her head when she masturbated, but now that she'd given in, she never wanted to let go of it.

"All right, stop, stop," Renee whispered, pushing Garza back against the wall. Her eyes were shining in the dark, and her hands were like vices on Garza's shoulders. "When I leave, wait ten minutes and follow me. I'll be waiting just outside the airport in my car. Get in the passenger side. I'll take you home. Okay?"

"Yes, ma'am."

Renee softly stroked Garza's cheek. Then she looked away to make sure no one else had wandered out from the hangar. Confirming they were alone, she kissed Garza one more time and then let go of her, walked away from her, marched back into the light and shouted to someone as if the last five minutes hadn't happened. Her skin felt like it had been flayed off, leaving only exposed nerves everywhere. She shuddered and took a moment to compose herself, buttoning her shirt before she followed Renee back into the hangar.

Inside, Renee had become Mrs. Barrett once more. She was their instructor, the woman who had spent the past few weeks teaching them everything they needed to know about a plane. "It's not just about what you do at the controls," she'd said at the beginning of the class. "It's about know what those controls do, and how they do it, and how to keep yourself alive when something goes wrong." She was strict, she was uncompromising, the kind of instructor who would praise you one second and then berate you for a mistake the next.

The transformation was so complete and convincing that Garza started to think maybe she'd hallucinated the entire exchange in the dark. Everything from Mrs. Barrett putting a hand on her shoulder and whispering, "Could I see you outside for a moment, Miss Garza?" to coming back inside was just a fantasy. It wouldn't have been the first fantasy she had about her instructor. But it would have certainly been the most vivid.

But then Renee bid everyone a good night and, at the door, caught Garza's eye. She held the stare for too long to be accidental, and then she was gone.

Garza waited ten minutes.

She excused herself.

She left the airport and found the car waiting by the side of the road. The engine was running, but the lights were off. Garza's heart was in her throat as it got closer... and closer... and she could see Renee's silhouette behind the wheel. She could keep walking. She knew that was an option. Her hands were sweating. She knew if she stopped walking, her knees would shake so hard she might fall down. Her mouth was bone dry.

She opened the passenger door and got into the car.

Renee didn't say anything. She put the car in gear and pulled away from the shoulder.

Fifteen minutes later, in Renee's bed, breathless from kissing, Garza realized they were close to the point of no return. This was going to happen. So she put her hand on top of Renee's, which had just finished unzipping her pants.

"I've never done this before."

"With a woman?"

Garza shook her head.

Renee smiled and kissed her, both of them keeping their eyes open as Renee slid her hand into Garza's underwear.

"Then I guess I still have a few lessons to each you, Erika Garza…"

She slapped herself across the face once, hard, to pull herself back into the present. Not enough sleep and lulled into a trance by the vivid memories and the unchanging landscape she was flying over. She couldn't get distracted by thoughts of Renee, or the disasters that came after. The slap reminded her of the last time they'd seen each other, the sharp pain of Renee's hand striking her cheek so hard that she had fallen back into her chair.

"How dare you?"

An invitation to join the flight school as an assistant. Renting Renee's guesthouse for convenience, but really so they could share a bed without raising too many eyebrows. It was amazing for a while. For nearly a whole year, Garza spent her days in and around planes and her nights in bed with a beautiful older woman who did things to her body she never imagined possible.

But then rumors started to swirl. A student kicked out of the class for reckless behavior and terrible grades complained that Renee had propositioned him. He said that she would've let him stay in the class in exchange for sexual favors. The school ran an investigation, during which Garza was asked to testify about her experiences with Renee.

"What is your relationship with Mrs. Barrett?"

Garza, mouth dry: "Sexual."

She'd planned to explain that Renee's sexual preference proved the other student was lying. She planned to use herself as an alibi to explain his claims were impossible. She couldn't have possibly propositioned him when she was humping Garza in the backseat of her car. But she didn't have a chance to explain any of that, because Renee immediately leapt from her seat and said, "That is a damn lie!"

In the end, Renee had been cleared of any inappropriate behavior. Garza was declared, both by the school and Renee herself, to have been conspiring with the student who first made the claims. *"Clearly paid or otherwise enticed to spread malicious rumors about Mrs. Barrett's behavior."*

Garza was fired and, when she cleaned out her office at the airport, she found a note from Renee informing her that she was also evicted from the guesthouse. She would need to find a new place to live.

The last time she saw Renee, she'd been leaving the guesthouse with the last box of her things. She'd thought Renee would be at the airport teaching a class. She turned around and saw her standing in the doorway, and she was so startled she dropped the box on her foot.

"I was trying to help," she said weakly.

Renee came into the room and stood in front of her. Garza had never seen her face so full of rage. She wanted to look away but she felt it was important to keep eye contact.

At least until the slap.

Garza had left town after that. Started over, opened her own charter airline. At the time it had been freeing. She'd felt completely gutted by how things ended, how suddenly Renee went from the center of her universe to a ghost, and she'd sleepwalked through the rough early days. When she finally came out of the darkness, her new life was underway. She didn't know if she had it in her to start over again if things with Parrish went downhill.

By the time she landed in Calgary, she'd made her decision. She refueled and settled in to wait for the time she'd told Saul she'd be waiting.

Sure enough, at half past five, she saw him strolling toward her across the tarmac. His briefcase was in one hand, the handle of his small overnight bag in the other. She went to the door to welcome him aboard and helped him with his luggage, such as it was.

"I appreciate the punctuality, Miss Garza," he said as he brushed by her.

"Well, I'll do my best to keep this level of customer service."

He looked at the co-pilot seat, then at the other passenger seats further back. He gestured at one of the aisle seats. "Would it be all right if I sat here? My intention is to sleep through most of the flight, and I don't wish to be a distraction to you."

She intuited that he meant he also didn't want *her* to disrupt him by moving around and flipping switches. She shrugged and gestured for him to take whatever seat he wanted.

"That's a good seat. It'll keep the sun out of your face." She then winced and said, "Or... it would... if we were traveling the other direction... uh, yeah, no, sit wherever. It's fine."

He nodded his thanks and settled into the middle seat on the starboard side. Garza went up front and took her station, grateful he was the one who made the decision not to sit next to her. It would cut down on the awkwardness to a huge degree. As she went through her pre-flight, she glanced back to see he was still awake and waiting patiently, hands folded on top of the briefcase in his lap.

"Did you have a good visit?" she asked.

He looked up, as if startled she was there or had the power of speech. "Yes. It was quite productive. And... you? Did you have a good week?"

"Oh, you know," Garza said. "Pretty quiet. Not much to do in a small town like Red Kite."

"You should call Christine. I imagine she gets quite bored all alone."

Garza was extremely grateful he wasn't sitting next to her. "Yeah," she finally managed to get out. "Maybe I'll do that."

***

Saul indeed managed to sleep for most of the flight back. Garza was more relaxed in his presence than she would have expected, given the anxiety she'd felt on the first leg of the trip. Maybe it would have been different if he was right next to her, or if he'd been conscious, but she was confident she could handle either of those scenarios if they presented themselves.

Her calm wavered a little when she saw the airport below her and realized Saul's car was parked next to the runway. Night had fallen while they were in the air, but she had security lights framing the corners of the airport property and lining the runway. Even in that artificial light with its long shadows, the tiny white dot next to the car was definitely Christine.

Garza's anxiety spiked. She'd spent so much time worrying about the time alone with Saul that she'd never considered being with *both* of them. The secret would hang over them like the sword of Damocles, dangling and read to slice at any moment. One wrong word, one look that lingered too long...

She couldn't worry about that. Worrying about that would make it manifest. So instead she cleared her throat and raised her voice.

"Mr. Oakhill!" She looked to see his head raise up, eyes open and alert. "We're coming in for a landing now. I didn't want you to be caught off guard when we hit the ground."

"I am grateful, Miss Garza."

Minutes later, they were on the ground. Business as usual, just as she'd done hundreds of times. She taxied to the hangar and saw Parrish in her periphery, walking to meet them.

Wonderful.

The plane came to a stop. Garza unfastened her seatbelt and stood up, retrieving Saul's bags. He took them from her with a nod of thanks and led the way off the plane.

"There you are," Parrish said as they came down the stairs.

She was in another long flowing dress, but this one barely existed above the waist. Her arms and shoulders were bare, the straps were just thin twists of string that looked like they could be undone by one firm tug. The bodice was also loosely tied, exposing far too much of her chest for polite company. Garza was distracted by the shine of sweat between her breasts. She could all too easily imagine licking it away. She couldn't stop herself from licking her lips at the sight, and she was grateful Saul was in front of her.

Parrish saw it, though. She threw her arms around Saul's neck and hugged him tightly. She put her chin against his shoulder and locked eyes with Garza. She ran her tongue over her top lip as if she'd read Garza's mind. Garza tensed and looked away, waiting for the hug to end. Saul, she noticed, kept one hand at his side, only returning the hug with his other. It was like he was greeting a cousin.

Garza cleared her throat. "If you'll follow me to the office, Mr. Oakhill, we can make arrangements for next week's trip."

He turned to her. "The same arrangement would works for me, unless you have objections. Departure early on Tuesday, return on Thursday evening."

"Works for me," Garza said.

Saul stepped back and put his arm across Parrish's shoulders, pulling her to his side. "I'm not sure I like the idea of my lady being out here after dark all alone waiting for me."

"Aw, you're sweet." Parrish put a hand on his chest and cuddled closer, chuckling under her breath. "I'm perfectly safe out here. Isn't that right, Miss... I'm sorry, it was..."

"Garza," she said, holding Parrish's gaze, then flicking a smile to Saul. "And she's right. She's perfectly safe when she's here, Mr. Oakhill. You have my word."

Saul smiled.

CHAPTER FIVE

Tuesday

Garza spent the weekend in the air as much as possible, giving her plenty of time to think about conventional wisdom. Sayings like 'absence makes the heart grow fonder.' Friday morning in her plane, flying two and a half hours to Winnipeg to deliver a case of coffee grounds, she could barely stop thinking about Parrish. Wanting to be with her, picturing her in various states of undress, imagining that barely-there dress she'd worn to pick up Saul and hating the fact she wasn't the one to peel away the strings to expose the skin beneath. She spent the entire flight wishing Parrish was next to her.

Then again, Saturday night, on a one-hour hop to drop off some fishermen in Moose Jaw, she found it was easier to distract herself when she was in the air. 'Out of sight, out of mind.' She didn't have to see the places in her home where Parrish had been, didn't have to relive the memory of those hours every time she looked at the bathtub or the tangled sheets of her bed. It was easier not to think about where she was, what she was doing, who she was with...

By Monday, she was torn between the two extremes. She wasn't thinking about Parrish, but she *was* horny. Going cold turkey after three days of almost constant sex had left her with an itch that masturbating just couldn't scratch. So Monday evening, after a flight to Regina, well aware that she would probably see Parrish the following day, she decided to find a bar on the right side of town and see what happened when she picked up a drink.

The woman she ended up talking to was a cop named Ann. She was cute, Lakota, with shining black hair that reached all the way to her waist when it was down. She wore a red blouse and blue jeans. She could not have been farther from the pale-haired, freckled, blue-eyed Christine Parrish if she'd tried. Garza only needed two glasses of beer to follow her down the hall to the bathroom.

When Ann came out, Garza put an arm on her shoulder and guided her toward the wall. She leaned in for a kiss. Ann put her hand on Garza's shoulder and chuckled nervously.

"What are you doing?"

Garza stepped back. "I thought..."

"This isn't one of those places," Ann said.

"I didn't... I-I was just..."

Ann looked into the barroom to make sure no one had seen, then patted Garza on the arm. "It's fine. We'll just pretend it didn't happen, okay?"

Garza agreed, disappointed but grateful Ann hadn't made more of a scene, and followed her back out to their seats.

They managed to finish their conversation - she was certain Ann wrapped things up much faster than she otherwise would have - and nursed the rest of her drink. For the entire walk back to the airport, she told herself she was fine to fly. It was just an hour back to Red Kite, and she wasn't that tired or drunk yet. She climbed into the plane and strapped herself into the pilot's seat. She took a deep breath, closed her eyes to prepare herself for the flight

...and woke to the sun shining in her eyes. "Shit," she muttered, touching the straps as her memory caught up with her brain. Definitely a good thing she hadn't flown, then. She wiped her hand over her face, wondering if she had time to pee or get some lunch. She checked the time. Eight forty-five. That wasn't too—

"*Shit.*"

Saul Oakhill's flight to Calgary was scheduled to leave at nine-thirty. Even if she was off the ground in the next thirty seconds, she'd be late. And *punctuality* was *so important* to him, she remembered him saying in that snooty voice of his.

She went into immediate panic mode. Her body started preparing for takeoff while her brain was still several steps behind. She would never know how she actually made it into the air - some combination of luck and muscle memory - but it was eight fifty-three the next time she looked at the clock. She was going to be half an hour late, maybe more judging by the wind, and then she would have to refuel the plane before she was able to take off, which added another half hour to the turn-around time. It would be fine. She could still get him to Calgary before lunchtime.

"It's fine," she said. "It'll be fine. It's fine."

She repeated the mantra for the entire trip, sweating and bouncing one knee to ignore the fact she really had to use the bathroom. As soon as she was back in control of her body, her head decided to let her know she was in store for a heck of a hangover. She could feel it brewing in the back of her skull but, without the opportunity to make herself a big greasy breakfast, all she could do was suffer.

As she'd feared, Saul's car was parked in front of the airport and the man himself was pacing down the length of the runway. Garza swore under her breath as she came in for her landing. Saul saw her coming and walked back toward the hangar. Even from the air, she could read the fury in his body language. She didn't see Parrish anywhere and hoped that meant she wouldn't be witness to whatever scolding he was about to give.

Saul approached the plane as soon as it came to a stop. She climbed out, her body demanding a bathroom, her hangover demanding an aspirin.

"Do you have any idea of the time, Miss Garza?" Saul snapped.

"Mr. Oakhill, if you would just give me two minutes to~"

"I have been waiting here for over an hour. I made it clear to you on our last trip that I value punctuality above all." He glared at his watch. "I demand we leave at once."

She held up her hands. "That's not going to be possible, Mr. Oakhill. There are a few things I need to do before we can get it back in the air~"

"Unacceptable! We have a contract in which you promised~"

"Jesus, Saul!"

They both turned toward the voice. Christine Parrish was walking toward them in a pale yellow skirt and a white tank top. She was wearing red cowboy boots, rolling her hips with every step. She took one hand off her hip to gesture at Garza as she glared at Saul.

"Can't you see the woman clearly needs a little time on solid ground?"

"We have a contract which agreed that my departing flights would leave at~"

"Would you rather spend the next two hours on a plane with a woman who wet her pants, or do you want to give her five minutes?"

Saul clenched his jaw and looked at Garza, then looked away.

Parrish had reached them. "Miss Garza, you do whatever you need to get done. I made sure you'd find something to eat in the kitchen."

"Thanks," Garza managed. "I do apologize for the delay, Mr. Oakhill."

He mumbled something, but Garza was moving too fast to hear it. She could tell the fight had gone out of him, if not the anger. It was going to be a tense flight, but the man was terrible company anyway. So no great loss there. She was unbuckling her pants as she entered the house, breathing heavily as she ran into the bathroom and kicked the door shut behind her.

A few minutes later, feeling reborn, she took the quickest sort of bath possible in the sink and changed into fresh clothes. Then she went into the kitchen and discovered where Parrish had been during the landing: a plate sat on the counter next to the stove with scrambled eggs, a sausage patty, and two pieces of toast. She groaned with gratitude and combined everything into a breakfast sandwich, which she ate as she headed out to begin refueling.

Saul and Parrish had retreated to their car. Parrish was still clearly chewing him out, and he looked appropriately chastened. Garza tried to ignore them as she went through the process of preparing to take the plane back out. She hated doing back to back legs like this, but she had no one to blame but herself. She should never have stuck around Regina.

She had almost finished when she saw Parrish had left the car and was making her way over. She moved to the far side of the plane, where Saul couldn't see them. Parrish came around the tail and joined her.

"Thanks for calming him down," Garza said.

"He acts like being late is a cardinal sin. Did you find your breakfast? I made you a plate."

"Found," Garza said. "Devoured. Very, very grateful."

"You're welcome. So where were you?"

"I'll tell you tonight." She paused. "I'm seeing you tonight, right?"

Parrish smiled, almost coy. It was a far cry from the predator she'd been last week. "Hell yeah," she said quietly. She reached out and brushed Garza's cheek. "I've missed you."

"I missed you, too."

The plane shook as Saul boarded. Parrish stepped away from Garza and put her hands behind her back, bowing her head to look down at the ground. Garza cleared her throat and moved back from the plane.

"We should get underway."

"Mm-hmm. Have a safe flight."

They went around the plane by separate routes, Parrish going back around the tail while Garza ducked under the propeller. Saul had left the door open and she climbed aboard, shutting the door behind her and securing it before she got into her seat.

"I wish to apologize for my behavior," Saul said.

"Don't worry about it," Garza said. "You weren't entirely wrong. I dropped the ball, you had every right to be angry."

He considered that. "Regardless, I regret the tone I used."

"It's forgiven."

"As is your tardiness."

She decided she could live with that. "The good news is that the wind will be with us into Calgary, so I might be able to make up a few minutes in the air."

"Do your best," he said.

Garza nodded and decided she'd do exactly that.

"Did you fuck him?"

There was a long enough pause before Parrish said, "Yes," that made it clear she'd considered lying.

They were in bed together, sweaty from their enthusiastic reunion sex. Garza spent the flight back certain that she would beg Parrish to give her a few hours for a nap, some real proper sleep in a bed to recover from her ill-advised layover in Regina. But then she'd walked into the house to find Parrish sitting on the kitchen table waiting for her. Those red boots were resting on one of the chairs. The skirt hung limp between her spread knees like an invitation.

"How do you keep getting in my house?" Garza asked as she closed the door behind her.

"It's not hard," Parrish said, sitting up straighter, putting her hands between her knees, which only drew Garza's attention back to her legs. "You probably want to get some rest."

"Yeah," Garza said. "I'm exhausted."

She pulled the chair away and stepped between Parrish's knees, reaching down to guide her into wrapping her legs around her waist. Parrish obliged, arms automatically wrapping around Garza's shoulders as their lips met. Garza pushed her down until her back was on the table, then kissed down her body. Her chest was sweaty, and Garza ran her tongue up her breastbone to her throat. She moaned; she could get drunk on the taste of that.

Parrish's nipples were hard, and Garza bit and sucked them through the thin material of her tank top. She tugged the tank from the waistband of the dress and kissed the exposed skin of her stomach, dipping her tongue into Parrish's belly button, making her gasp and squirm.

And then she lifted Parrish's skirt, and Parrish reached down to move it out of her way. Parrish put her hands on top of her leg, and her legs were now on her shoulders, so Garza felt she had no option but to finish what she'd started. It was only after Parrish came and Garza sat up to kiss her that she realized Parrish hadn't been wearing panties.

"Was that a set-up?" she'd asked as Parrish led her to the bedroom.

"Well. I *was* willing to let you sleep," Parrish said. "But now I have a debt to repay to you first."

Garza groaned and slumped her shoulders as she was pulled down onto the bed. "This day is never going to end..."

Now, after the sex, more exhausted than when she'd arrived, Garza still couldn't stop herself from asking the question that had been circling at the back of her mind. And she'd known the answer was yes. Of course it was yes. Parrish had never implied they didn't have a sex life, just that it wasn't fulfilling. She'd had to ask, but now she regretted having her suspicions confirmed.

Parrish pushed herself up on her elbow and gazed down at her. "Are you upset?" Her hair had fallen across her face when she sat up. She tucked it behind her ear. "Is that going to be a problem?"

"No." Garza reached up and traced her finger down the center of Parrish's chest. "I tried to fuck someone else, too."

"Oh really?" Parrish said, eyebrows rising. "How'd that go?"

"Not well. That's the reason I was late. I don't want to talk about it."

Parrish put her hand on Garza's stomach. "Is this going to be a problem? Because you know I don't plan on leaving Saul. And if you're~"

"I'm not," Garza said. "I'm not clingy or needy or any of that shit. I've just never done anything like this before. It's going to take a second for my brain to catch up. But it will."

Parrish looked skeptical, but she nodded. She scooted down a little in the bed so she could put her head on Garza's chest.

"It was the wording."

"What?"

"You asked if I fucked him. If you'd asked if we had sex, or made love, I would've said no. But... you said... did *you*... fuck... *him*. And that's what happened. I initiated it. He... consented, I guess would be the best word for it. But then everything that happened afterward was me doing what needed to be done so I could get off. What you and I do? That's so different it doesn't even feel like the same word covers it. Do you know he's never gone down on me?"

"What?' Garza looked down to see if Parrish was joking. "How long have you been together?"

"Six years."

"*What! And he's never...?*"

"He tried a couple of times at the beginning," she sighed. "I practically begged him for it. But it was... he... Well..." She held up two fingers and pressed a series of dry, closed-mouth kisses to where they were pressed together. "Imagine that, but the whole time he's making a face like he's doing a chore."

"You said he liked using his mouth. Oh. Oh, right." She made a face, realizing what Parrish had meant when she said that. She shook her head. "God. What a nightmare. I know you said it gives you security and a place to live, but that's just... I don't know. I don't want to judge."

Parrish stroked her fingers over Garza's breast, circling her nipple until it hardened. She moved her head so she could take it into her mouth and suck gently. Garza grunted, closed her eyes, and played with Parrish's hair.

"Okay, point taken," she said. "We don't have to talk about him."

"No. It's only right that you should get to ask questions." She brushed her thumb over Garza's nipple. "If it ever gets to be too much for you... tell me. I don't know what I'll do, but I'll figure something out. I know we've only been doing this for a week, but I don't want to lose... a-and I can't leave him. I'd be losing everythi~"

Garza looked down at her. Parrish's eyes were wide open, her face more vulnerable than she'd ever seen it.

"Hey." Parrish looked up at her, and Garza shook her head. "I meant it. We don't have to talk about him at all."

Relief washed over Parrish's face. "Are you sure?"

"Yeah. It can wait. Ghost days. You and me, fuck the rest of the world. Right now it can... it can just be fun." She smiled. "And it's been *very* fun."

Parrish laughed and stretched to kiss Garza's lips. "Very fun. Thank you." She kissed her again, a little longer this time. "But you know what will be more fun?"

"Sleep?"

Parrish smiled and bumped her nose against Garza's. "We can have more fun when you wake up."

Garza closed her eyes, knowing she was going to hold Parrish to that promise.

CHAPTER SIX

Wednesday

Someone knocked on the front door, then rang the buzzer. Garza was woken up by the knock, but she didn't start moving until the buzzer. She kicked the covers away from her feet, pulled on a pair of pants, and was struggling her way into a T-shirt by the time Parrish sat up and rubbed her eyes in confusion.

"Wussa?" she slurred through still sleep-tangled lips.

"Customer, I'm thinking," Garza said, putting her hand on Parrish's shoulder to guide her back down. "Go back to sleep."

She threw a button-down shirt on over her T-shirt and made her way to the business side of the house, still blinking the sleep out of her eyes. The clock in the kitchen told her it was a little after eight o'clock in the morning. She and Parrish had spent another long night doing everything they could do in a bed that didn't include sleeping. She was starting to wonder if it counted as restful sleep if she was just passing out from exhaustion every night. It definitely couldn't be healthy.

A large man was waiting outside. He'd paced away from the building, hands on his hips, lips twisted in a sneer and eyes squinted shut as he looked toward the road. Garza cleared her throat, ignored the fact she was barefoot, and made sure she was presentable before she opened the door. The man turned and his face softened just a little. She vaguely recognized him from town but didn't know him.

"Edmonton?"

"Uh, Erika Garza," she said. "Owner, operator, pilot of Red Kite Aviation. How~"

"Do you *fly* to *Edmonton?*" he said. "Got a baseball team down there, left bags with all their uniforms on my bus. Acting like it's *my* problem, like *I've* got to give up a whole day just to drive it back. Told them I might be able to arrange for a pilot to take it. You get the bags there by two this afternoon, they'll cover your fees."

Garza processed all the information he'd just dumped on her. She focused on the numbers and nodded. "Yeah. I can get to Edmonton by two. No problem."

"Fantastic." He pulled a card from his pocket and wagged it at her. "I'll get the bags out of the truck. Let me know how much it's gonna set them back and I'll call the manager, let him know you're on the way."

"Sure," Garza said. "Yeah, okay."

He turned and shuffled back to his truck. Garza reached up and smoothed down her hair, going to her desk. She worked up receipt, along with a note for the bus driver - his card revealed his name was Billy Boward - so he could convey the price to the team manager. He came back with four big bags and information about who she was supposed to meet at the Edmonton airport. The bags were bigger than she expected, but she would have plenty of room for them if she put a couple in the passenger seats of the plane. She thanked Billy and set the bags by the door to take them out to the plane when she was ready.

Once he was back in his truck and driving away, Garza returned to the bedroom. Parrish was on her stomach, hugging the pillow. It looked like she had tried to stay awake until Garza returned but failed, her face relaxed and lips hanging slack. Garza smiled and crouched down next to the bed so their faces lined up.

"Christine," she whispered.

A flinch, then a blink, and then beautiful blue eyes locked on hers. And a smile. Garza would remember that smile. "Hi," Parrish said.

"Hi," Garza said. "Wanna go see a baseball game?"

Parrish raised an eyebrow.

***

Parrish had jumped at the opportunity once Garza explained the job. "You wanted to go out and get a drink or whatever," Garza said, "but I was worried about people seeing us. I figure this way, we get the best of both worlds. Spend time among people without worrying we might run into someone we know." Parrish enthusiastically agreed and immediately began dressing. She asked if she had time to go home so she could change into something more appropriate for a game and Garza confirmed she did. She kissed Garza on the cheek and was out of the house and driving away quicker than seemed possible.

While she was gone, Garza took a bath and washed away the incredibly hectic previous day. It felt like this was her first chance to breathe since waking up in a panic on Tuesday. Being with Parrish was a fun kind of frenzy, but she was grateful for the reprieve. She cupped her hands under the water and brought it up over her head, dousing herself, then brushed her wet hand over her face.

Parrish had brought up a very good point. What they had was only a week old. She couldn't be this attached, this jealous, craving this much of Parrish's time because of deeper feelings. She was just horny. And jealous that someone else had been spending time with Parrish when they could've been together. That was all it was. She and Parrish were just pals hanging out, usually naked. She wouldn't put extra weight on what they had just because it was new.

When she heard Parrish coming back in the car, she got out of the tub and wrapped the towel around herself as she walked into the bedroom. She'd changed into a sundress with lilies on it. She was carrying a wide-brimmed straw hat and a pair of large sunglasses, which she pushed down to admire the sight of Garza, who was still in her underwear.

"Hi," she said. "Is that what you're wearing? I love it."

"I thought maybe I'd go with something a little less scandalous."

Parrish shrugged. "Your choice." She walked to the bed and put down her hat and glasses before she sat on the tangled sheets. She watched Garza walk back to the closet and go through her options. "Hey, can I make a request?"

"Sure."

"Can you dress like a man?"

Garza said, "As opposed to my usual evening gown and stilettos?"

"No, I mean…" She got up and joined Garza at the closet. "You said you dress the way you do because it's comfortable and convenient. But…" She took out a tie and draped it around Garza's neck like a tie. "Can you actually dress like you're pretending to be a man? Just for today. So when we're out at the game or whatever, I don't have to worry about who might see us holding hands or, or whatever. I don't know. It's a dumb idea."

"No, it's not," Garza said. "I get it. I think I have some stuff that will work."

Parrish smiled. "Yeah?"

"Yeah, let me look."

She ended up wearing a tight white undershirt that held down her breasts enough to slim down her profile, then a button-down shirt and tie. She had been planning to wear slacks anyway, so she chose a pair she thought looked most masculine and tucked the shirt into them. She smoothed down the material and turned to let Parrish look her over.

"What do you think?"

"Very handsome," Parrish said. "Saul left his fedora in the car. If it fits, you can use it."

"I have—"

"I want you to wear his," Parrish interrupted.

Garza nodded. She could spend the flight analyzing that request, if she decided she cared enough to dig deeper on it.

She went to the bathroom and looked in the mirror. Not too bad if no one looked very closely. She would have to speak to whoever she handed the bags to at the airport, but they didn't need to believe the ruse. It would be easy to blend into the crowd once they were at the game. Parrish came into the bathroom behind her. She put her arms around Garza's waist and rested her chin on her shoulder.

"Handsome," she said.

"Yeah?" Garza smiled and leaned back against Parrish. She turned her head and pecked Parrish's cheek. "I just need to do a few more things and then I'll be ready to go. In the meantime, we have time for a late breakfast or an early lunch if you want to make something."

Parrish stepped away and slapped Garza's ass. "Okay. I'll see what's in the kitchen. Let's get a move on, Captain."

Garza laughed, straightened the knot on her tie, and headed out to prepare the plane.

Edmonton was a two and a half hour flight, almost as long as it took to get to Calgary. Even though it was three hundred miles north, Garza could almost feel the distance between them and Saul shrinking. She put him out of her mind as much as she could to focus on her day with Parrish. It was just going to be a baseball game, maybe dinner afterward, but it would be the closest thing she had to a date in ages, and she intended to fully appreciate it.

The manager of the baseball team was waiting at the airport, checkbook in hand. He paid for the flight as Parrish helped by loading the bags into the backseat of his truck.

"I swear, the gods don't want us playing in this game," he said as he signed the check. "First our bus breaks down and we take the only one that will get us here today. Then my damn fool equipment manager forgets the uniforms. I don't even want to think what might happen at the game."

"You know," Parrish said, "I haven't been to a baseball game in forever. Think we might tag along back with you? See if we can get a couple tickets?"

"Plenty of tickets to be had, no worries about that. Sure, the truck's got room. Hop in."

As Garza suspected from the ordeal the manager had detailed, the ballpark was barely more than a fenced-in field with metal risers serving as the bleachers. A handful of players from the team - inexplicably called the Stoneham Vendors - were waiting outside to take the bags into the locker room. The manager thanked Garza and Parrish again, then hurried after the players.

They got their tickets and headed to their seats. Garza felt horribly awkward and self-aware, but she knew focusing on that would only make it worse. No one would pay any attention to her unless she started acting squirrely. So she just relaxed and took her seat on the metal bench next to Parrish.

"This was a really great idea," Parrish said.

"Can't take all the credit. Just jumped at the opportunity." She looked around for signs of concessions. Hot dogs or popcorn or beer. "I'm just glad it happened on the right day."

"Mm-hmm."

Parrish reached over and took Garza's hand, pulling it to her and resting their linked fingers in her lap. Garza forced herself not to look around to see who might see. They were just two people seeing a game together, that was all. No one would care unless she gave them a reason to look closer. She moved her feet a little further apart, spreading her knees wider, and tried to affect what she considered to be a manly slouch.

"This is probably going to be a godawful game," Garza said.

"Did I hear right?" Parrish asked. "They're called the Vendors?"

"The Stoneham Vendors, yeah."

"Where is that?"

Garza laughed and shook her head. "Couldn't tell you."

Parrish grinned and leaned against her. "Maybe the other team will be better."

"Maybe."

The Stoneham Vendors were as lousy as their name implied. Their opponents, the Edmonton Klondikers, were even worse. It was probably the most terrible baseball game Garza had ever seen in her entire life. It was lucky, then, that sometimes the wind caught the hem of Parrish's dress and lifted it to show off her thigh. And sometimes Parrish would shift on the bleacher and cross one leg over the other, and Garza got to watch that process happen. So all in all, worth the price of the ticket and the snacks she bought during the nine interminable innings.

The game ended at five o'clock, a blessing. The manager who had given them a ride to the park was nowhere to be seen, and Garza spent a horrible few minutes unsure how they would get back to the airport. She decided to delay the problem a bit and suggested they walk to the fried chicken restaurant she'd seen a few blocks away from the park.

After they got their food, Parrish impulsively decided to swap hats. She put Saul's fedora on the crown of her head so her hair stuck out at the front, the brim pointed jauntily into the air.

"You look good in that hat," Garza said.

"I look good in everything."

Garza gave her that point.

Parrish looked past her to the checkout line. "Oh, hold on just a second." She stood up, smoothed down her dress, and pushed back her shoulders to highlight her breasts. She walked up to a man in mechanic overalls and smiled as she lightly touched his arm. "Sorry, excuse me, sir. I noticed the logo on your back here. Are you by chance on your way to work at the airport?"

His eyes went to her cleavage first, then guiltily moved up to her eyes. "Um, yes, ma'am..."

"That's *great!*" Parrish said, bouncing on the balls of her feet in a way that made her body do interesting, distracting things under the dress. "My friend and I lost our ride, and we just need a lift. We'd be happy to wait for you to have your meal, and we'll pay for it, even, if you'd be willing to take us."

"Oh, well, uh." He was blushing brightly. "Well, you don't have to pay nothin'. I'm going there anyway. If you need to get there, I'd be more than happy."

Parrish squeezed his arm. "Ah! Our hero. Thank you..." She looked at his name patch. She poked it with two fingers as if pressing a button. "Thomas! Our hero, Thomas. You're a lifesaver."

"Oh geez, I dunno about that," he said bashfully.

"We'll be right over there whenever you're ready. No rush!"

She walked back to the table, somehow making the hem of her dress sway like a broom being swept back and forth before she dropped down into her seat. Garza had watched the entire interaction with eyebrows raised, and now she rested her chin on her fist.

"Who *are* you?"

Parrish winked. "Someone who knows how to get what she wants."

The mechanic, Thomas, was quick to finish his meal. Not that Garza blamed him, after the show Parrish had put on. He was driving an old tow truck, and this time Garza sat between him and Parrish. She didn't want the poor fool getting any ideas.

When he dropped them off at the terminal, he twisted in the seat and looked past her at Parrish.

"So, uh, I-I'm happy to… help… if you… I mean, if you need anything else, anything at all…"

Garza could almost hear his thoughts processing what he really wanted to say. She almost felt sorry for him, even as she shrank back into the seat. It was like she had ceased to exist, and it was just him and Parrish in the cab.

"Gosh, you're sweet!" Parrish put her hand on Garza's thigh, seemingly casual but far too close to her hip to be anything but suggestive, and leaned across her to place a lingering kiss on Thomas' cheek. "Mwah! My hero."

His face was bright crimson. "Well, any time you're in town, ma'am."

"I'll keep you in mind. Thank you!"

She winked and opened the door, hoping out onto the sidewalk. Garza awkwardly lifted her hand to wave goodbye, then scooted sideways until she was also out of the truck. They watched the truck as it trundled off to whichever hangar required his services. Parrish stretched to her full height, arm extended over her head so she could wave until he was out of sight.

Garza snickered and shook her head. "You wouldn't manipulate me like that, would you?"

"I don't know," Parrish said coyly. "Is there anything I want that you haven't freely given me?"

"Hm," Garza said, unsure if she was teasing or hinting at something.

She decided she could twist her brain around that question until she couldn't think straight, so she just dropped it and started walking back to the plane. Parrish followed her like a shadow.

When they were aboard the plane, Parrish watched every movement of Garza's hands. Every switch she flipped, the dials she turned, the gauges she checked.

"How much does gas cost for a thing like this?" she asked.

"You really don't want to know."

"Ouch?"

"Ouch," Garza agreed. "Most of the client's fee goes right into the tank. Everything left over usually goes to upkeep or some kind of repair. That's just how it works. But I didn't get into this for the money. Thank goodness."

Parrish grinned.

They'd been in the air for half an hour when Parrish, who had been watching the terrain pass under them, suddenly unfastened her seatbelt.

"Where do you think you're going?"

"Nowhere," Parrish said. "I just had an idea."

"What~"

Parrish lifted her hips to pull her dress up, then sat down again to pull the dress over her head. She dropped the dress in the space between their seats. Garza was still processing that when Parrish's hips lifted again and she slid her panties down her legs and kicked them off. Her bra came next, landing on top of the panties. Now completely naked except for her shoes and socks, she fastened herself back into her seat and gave a sigh of relief.

"Much better," she said.

"What..." Words failed her. "You can't be naked on a plane."

Parrish shrugged. "Why not? No one out there is going to see us. And the only other person here is you, and you've already seen everything."

"I... I..."

"You've never flown naked?"

Garza said, "No!"

Parrish turned toward her. "Do it now."

"No!"

"Why not?"

Garza didn't have an answer better than 'because.'

"C'mon, Erika. Take off your clothes for me."

A shiver ran down her spine. "You're playing me now. Just like that poor mechanic."

"The difference is, I'll actually fuck you if you play along."

Garza took a deep breath and let it out, then shook her head. "You're evil." She let go of the yoke and unfastened her seatbelt.

Parrish grinned and clapped her hands quietly. She brought her hands to her face so she could chew on a thumbnail as Garza stood and quickly shed her pants and underwear. She sat down again to undo her tie, looking over at Parrish to make sure she was at least enjoying the show. Her eyes were wide and sparkling with light from the instrumental panel, and Garza sighed.

"Okay. So we're flying naked."

"Yeah!"

"Never done that before."

Parrish said, "Really? Why not?" She gestured at the empty seats behind them. "Like I said, no one here to see. And it's not like another plane is going to pass in the other direction and see us." She frowned and leaned forward to look out the windshield. "Right?"

"Right," Garza reluctantly admitted. "But it's still... weird. Like walking around the house naked. It's public space, you know? You never know what might happen. What if the plane crashes right now and they find our bodies naked?"

"That sounds like a fun story for the emergency workers."

Garza rolled her eyes, but she couldn't help smiling. "You're impossible. You've probably driven around in your car naked."

Parrish faced forward without responding.

"Oh my god. You *have*."

"Sometimes the risk of being caught makes it better," she said with a shrug. She stretched her arms over her head. "It's freeing.. It's not giving a shit and just enjoying the air on your skin. If you've only ever been naked in your bedroom and the bath, then you're not really living. Relax. Enjoy it. You might find out you like it."

Garza said, "That's what I'm worried about. I don't want to make this a habit."

"Every business needs a gimmick," Parrish said.

Garza laughed.

Despite her misgivings, Garza did eventually relax and settle back into her seat. The tight T-shirt she'd been wearing to try concealing her breasts had been incredibly uncomfortable. Now she felt like she could breathe properly for the first time all day. And when she tested it by taking a deep breath, in her periphery she caught Parrish turning to check her out. She smiled and decided while flying naked definitely wasn't for her, she could deal with it for one flight in the right company.

When they were fifteen minutes out, Garza said, "We should probably get our clothes back on."

Parrish looked outside. "It'll be dark by the time you land. If we're quick..."

"I'm not risking that," Garza said firmly.

"Fine, fine," Parrish said with an exaggerated sigh.

She reached down to the pile between them. She had to move Garza's clothes out of the way to get to her dress, but she paused and fingered the material. After a second, she picked up the pants and stood to put them on. Garza frowned at her.

"What are you doing?"

"Putting on your clothes."

"What will I~"

"My dress."

Garza looked down at the dress. She didn't generally like dresses. No pockets. Who would invent clothes without pockets? It was insane. But she supposed she could wear one briefly. Just for a quick walk from the hangar to the house. She looked at Parrish, who was now buttoning her blouse with the tie draped across her shoulders. And she *did* look damn good in Garza's clothes...

She sighed and picked up the dress. At least it was easier to put on without standing up. She pulled the material over her head, tugging it into place. She didn't bother with underwear. She assumed it would get taken off again immediately once they got home anyway. She raised up out of the seat and pulled the dress all the way into place, smoothing the hem over her thighs.

"I feel like I'm in a nightgown."

Parrish looked at her and laughed. "That is *definitely* not your color."

"Well, hopefully no one will see me in it before you take it off me."

"Can't wait," Parrish said, fiddling with the tie. "How do you tie one of these things?"

"Don't worry about it. It looks good loose."

Parrish said, "Hm," and dropped her hands.

As they passed over Red Kite, Garza pulled slightly to the north to give Parrish a better view. "There she is. Home sweet home."

"Wow." Parrish leaned forward. "I've never seen the town like this. It looks like, um... like one of those little railroad toys. I can see people! And cars! Wow."

Garza grinned. "Yeah, it never gets old."

Parrish settled back in her seat. "I'm sure that's true. But I've never been up in a plane before."

"Really?"

Parrish shrugged. "It's expensive. Cheaper to just go everywhere by car or train. Bus."

"You should've said something. I would have taken a more scenic route."

"Oh, it was plenty scenic."

Garza laughed and wiped her hand over her face, hoping it concealed her blush.

They were almost home when Parrish said, "He never would've done this, you know. Saul."

"What, worn your dress?"

Parrish laughed, but it lacked the life the sound usually had. "No, I mean... all of this. Today. Woken me up to spend the day going to a terrible baseball game with teams we've never heard of and eating greasy chicken for dinner. He would have... he would have found articles about the teams and found out which game would be the most statistically important, and he would plan to go see *that* one, even if it was six hundred miles away, and he'd have a plan about how to get back to the airport that didn't involve flirting with strangers, and the whole day would have had a schedule and..." She realized she was ranting and stopped herself, covering her mouth with her hand to stop the words.

Garza waited. "Are you okay?"

"Mm-hmm." Parrish sniffled. "Sorry. Today was perfect."

"Good," Garza said. "I'm glad you had a good time. I did, too."

Parrish smiled.

Garza set the plane down as gently as possible, now that she knew it was Parrish's first trip in a plane. They walked together to the house, and Garza felt the weight of the day starting to drag on her. She reached out and took Parrish's hand, linking their fingers, and Parrish swung their arms.

When they got inside, Garza left the light off and pulled Parrish to her with a quiet, "Come here." They kissed in the dark, feet shuffling across the floor toward the hallway, or a wall, or a counter, something solid they could use for support so the kiss could become something more. Parrish whimpered into Garza's mouth, pulling her close, slipping her tongue across Garza's lips as she was guided backward through the house.

When they reached the bedroom, Garza pushed Parrish down onto the bed. "Scoot up," she said, pulling her borrowed dress over her head in one smooth movement. She tossed it aside as Parrish repositioned herself with her head on the pillow. She unfastened her belt and opened her pants, and Garza pulled them down her legs, dropping them into the floor as Parrish unbuttoned her shirt.

Garza climbed onto the bed, straddling Parrish's waist. She grabbed the tie that still hung loose around her neck and pulled it free.

"Put your arms over your head," she said.

"What?" Parrish said, still unbuttoning her shirt.

"Arms over your head," Garza said again. "Wrists crossed."

Parrish raised her head to see the iron bars of the headboard. She looked at Garza again, eyes wide. "Really?"

"Would Saul do this?"

"Never."

"Then put your arms up for me, Christine."

Parrish did as she was told, crossing her wrists like an X. It took Garza a second to figure out how to loop the tie so that it covered both arms and went around the bar, but she managed it. She knotted the tie and slid down, lined her face up with Parrish's, and kissed her hard. Parrish squirmed under her, and she lifted her head off the pillow in pursuit when Garza ended the kiss.

"What happens now?" Parrish said.

Garza sat up. Parrish had left the top three buttons of the shirt buttoned, so Garza grabbed the material and yanked until they popped off. She let the two halves fall open to expose Parrish's breasts, which she cupped with both hands. Parrish lifted up off the bed to press them into Garza's palms.

"You don't have to worry about that, darlin'," Garza said, her voice husky with want. "I'm going to do all the work tonight. And you're just going to lie there and enjoy it."

Parrish writhed under her. "God, you spoil me."

Garza grinned and slid down Parrish's body, her exhaustion faded as she started coming up with a list of things she wanted to do with her willing captive.

It happened accidentally. A busy, exhausting day followed by enthusiastic sex had left Garza physically drained. And preparing for another weekend without seeing, touching, tasting, holding Parrish was weighing on her emotionally. So after she made Parrish come twice, and after Parrish's hands had been freed so she could return the favor, and after they settled into a clinch on one side of the bed with the sheets tangled around them like a nest, Parrish kissed Garza's throat, her lips lingering on the pulse, and Garza slipped up.

"I love you," she whispered into Parrish's hair.

There was no response from the lips still resting against her throat. And despite how tired she was, Garza lay awake for another hour wondering if Parrish had heard her, hoping she'd been asleep by the time the words slipped free, wishing she could take them back, hating that she had to.

CHAPTER SEVEN

Thursday

The next morning, Parrish woke up first. She was sitting on the edge of the bed, facing out into the room with her feet on the floor. Garza eyed the smooth line of her back, split down the center by a rocky spine, looking for evidence of bruises either fresh or fading. There was nothing, and she was absolutely grateful for that, but she hated that she looked. She hated looking for signs of abuse, hated trying to find a reason to hate Saul for reasons beyond his selfishness and bland personality. She wanted him to be a monster. She wanted him to be cruel beyond withholding physical affection. If he was objectively despicable, Garza could position herself as the hero of their story, instead of someone who was just taking what she wanted.

"I don't know if you heard what I said last night~"

"I heard it," Parrish said, having jumped slightly when Garza spoke.

Garza sat up. "Okay. Well, I wanted you to know, uh, we don't have to talk about it. I know I shouldn't have said it." She picked at the sheet, watching her fingers to stop trying to read Parrish's body language. "After everything yesterday, I was just... exhausted. It slipped out."

Parrish looked over her shoulder. "So you didn't mean it?"

Garza started to answer, then closed her mouth. She shrugged. "If it's easier."

"No, I'm asking you." She turned fully on the bed, facing Garza. "Did you mean it?"

Garza forced herself to meet Parrish's gaze. "Yeah."

Parrish looked down again. "That's not going to make me leave him."

"I know," Garza said. "I didn't say it to make you do anything. I said it because it's how I feel. And it's always nice to hear, and after everything you've told me, I think it's probably been a long time since anyone has said it to you. I wanted to be the one who said it."

Parrish rubbed at one eye with a knuckle.

"So fuck it," Garza said. "I love you. Intentional, wide awake, and when I'm positive you can hear it. It doesn't have to mean anything beyond what it means. Okay?"

Parrish nodded. "Thank you. Oh god." She looked up, her face twisted in disgust. "What a horrible response. I l—"

"No," Garza leaned forward and put her hand over Parrish's mouth. "Don't. You don't have to say it, and I don't want to hear it if you're not totally sure. Thank you works. I'm happy with thank you."

"Are you sure?"

Garza nodded. "Positive."

Parrish got back into bed and put her arms around Garza. She kissed her lightly, then again, and then harder.

"Will you make love to me?"

Garza lowered Parrish to the mattress.

Parrish was in a sour mood the rest of the morning. She put on her dress, then silently sat with her head down on the dinner table while Garza made them breakfast. She tried not to take it personally. She knew it didn't have anything to do with their conversation, but she couldn't help but feel the brunt of responsibility as they sat silently at the table picking at their food. She didn't want to take it back. She didn't want Parrish to say anything she wasn't prepared to say. But she hated that saying it, as good as it had felt, seemed to have sent what they had crashing into a wall at full speed.

"What time do you have to leave?" Parrish asked.

"Around noon."

Parrish made a quiet noise of affirmation. "I should probably head out around then, too."

"Okay," Garza said.

Parrish put her hand on her coffee mug, let go, then grabbed it again. She held it, but didn't take a drink. She just stared at it as if trying to figure out what the purpose of the thing was.

"You don't have to go get him."

"I do," Garza said. "It's my job."

Parrish looked at her. "I can break your plane."

"They have buses. There are other planes."

"It could give us another few hours."

Garza pushed back her chair and went to the kitchen. She crouched in front of the sink and dug around underneath until she found what she was looking for. She came back to the table and placed the wrench next to Parrish's plate, like it was part of the place setting.

"Try not to break anything too expensive," Garza said as she sat back down.

Parrish managed a weak smile at that. "Four days with him," she said, gingerly tracing the edge of the handle with her fingertip. "Four days I could be spending with you instead."

Garza didn't know what to say to that. She wasn't the one who had suggested this arrangement. She hadn't offered, hadn't hinted, hadn't opened up the possibility. She felt a deep-down irritation that Parrish was playing the victim situation in this when she had all the power. She could leave Saul. Just walk away, since they weren't married, and be with someone who made her happy. But apparently her priorities were different. But she couldn't say that to someone she'd just declared her love for. She refused to further sully the last few hours they had together with a fight.

So instead, she said, "I'll be here when it's over."

Parrish pushed her coffee away and stood up. "I'm going to go take a bath. If that's okay."

"Of course."

Parrish bent down and kissed the top of Garza's head. "Thank you, Erika."

Garza watched her go, then looked down at the food left on her plate. She suddenly didn't have much of an appetite.

***

Saul had such a punchable face, that she was surprised she hadn't lashed out at it before. She greeted him with a smile, a nod, and then followed him aboard the plane. He took one of the back seats again and Garza was happy to have him out of her sight. She was also grateful he wouldn't sit in the seat that had last held Christine Parrish's bare ass. Two hours to get him home, and then a thousand years until Parrish was in her bed again.

They were an hour into the flight when Saul spoke up. "Excuse me, Miss Garza."

"Everything all right?" she asked without turning around.

"There..." He hesitated. She looked back at him, and he aimed a long thin finger at the underside of her seat. "There seems to be a pair of... undergarments..."

Garza's heart leapt into her throat. She reached down, fishing around until she felt them, and pulled them free. She balled them up and dropped them into her lap.

"So that's where they went." She was surprised at how calm and normal she sounded. "Delivered a parcel of clothes to... a group of... fishermen... up in Medicine Hat." She had no idea where these words were coming from, but she was grateful for each of them. "One of the bags split open. I thought I got everything, but one of the wives said there were some items missing. Guess we just found one of them."

She smirked. She almost believed it herself.

"I see," he said. "I was sure there'd be a reasonable explanation. It was quite an unusual sight."

She forced a laugh. "Yeah, I bet."

She looked down at the wadded-up underwear in her lap. Parrish's. Of course they were. She clenched her jaw, wondered if Saul was the type of man who would recognize his partner's panties or if he would just think they all looked the same. Probably the latter. Hopefully the latter. Either way, she wasn't going to give him another chance to get a look at them. She palmed the cotton and shoved the panties into her pocket.

Hopefully the horrified panic would fade and the story would be funny by the time she had a chance to tell the story to Parrish.

***

Garza was so focused on landing safely that she didn't notice anything amiss, even after they were on the ground. Parrish's panties burned in her pocket, and she was certain Saul had spent the rest of the flight staring at them, seeing through the material of her pants to examine them to prove his suspicions. She landed, eager to be rid of him and the tension in her shoulders. He gathered his bags and waited for her to open the plane door for him. When he stepped out, he paused and looked toward the house, then toward the street.

"Curious," he said.

Garza, crouched and waiting to follow him off the plane, tensed. What had he seen? "What's that?" she asked.

"I assumed Christine would be waiting for me as she was last week."

Garza frowned. She straightened, looking out the window. When Parrish left, she'd implied she would come back to give him a lift home. It was only their second week doing this, so it wasn't like they had a routine, but it still seemed very odd.

"Maybe she lost track of time," Garza said. "Or she forgot what day it was."

"Perhaps." He continued out of the plane, finally freeing Garza as well. As they crossed to the house, he turned at the waist to look back at her. "May I use your telephone?"

Garza nodded. "Sure, no problem."

She unlocked the office and went behind the desk, lifting the phone and moving it to the other side of the desk for him. She sat awkwardly as he dialed, then turned her attention to the window. She wondered if Parrish's absence was because of her. Because of the conversation they'd had earlier. Her skin felt hot but, at the same time, she was radiating coldness from the inside, terrified Saul was about to find out about them. What if Parrish was at home, packing her things? She didn't dare let herself hope for that.

But if it didn't had anything to do with their affair, then where the hell was she?

"Hm."

She looked at Saul as he hung up. "No answer?"

"Perhaps she is on her way." He looked toward the road as if the car would appear there.

Garza nodded. "That's probably it. Long line at the bank or something. I'm sure she'll roll up any minute now."

Saul drummed his fingers on the receiver. "I won't wait. May I use your phone again?"

"Yeah, go ahead."

He dialed again. This time the call was answered almost immediately. "Yes, this is Saul P. Oakhill. I require a taxi." He gave them the address, reading it off one of the business cards on the desk. "Yes, the airport. Thank you." He put the phone back in its cradle. "A car will arrive in approximately fifteen minutes. I will wait outside."

"You can wait in~"

"I've disturbed your business enough." He picked up his luggage. "Thank you for your help."

He was gone before she thought of anything to say. He sat down on a bench outside, posture perfect, bags at his feet, and waited. Garza alternated between watching him and the road. Every minute that passed made it less and less likely any car would ever appear on the road. Even the taxi would somehow be swallowed up by this odd day.

But finally, just over ten minutes later, she saw someone coming. Parrish, she thought, at last. Saul would use the phone again to call the taxi company and cancel. But that would be fine. Maybe Parrish would wait outside when he made the call, and Garza would go to her so they could speak briefly while he was on the phone. She was dying to know why she'd been so late. Maybe it was a simple explanation, something innocuous like she'd guessed. Long line at the store, delay at the bank. Maybe she'd gone home to take a nap and her alarm didn't go off. She hadn't gotten very much sleep the night before, and yesterday had been busy.

Maybe... maybe she didn't want to come back here after their talk that morning. Maybe she forced Saul to call a cab on purpose so she wouldn't have to see Garza again.

The approaching car was the taxi. Her heart and stomach fell, revealing to her just how much she'd been hoping to see Parrish, even briefly. Even if they would've had to be casual and distant to each other, she'd been looking forward to it as one last glimpse before the drought of the long weekend.

Saul had also seen the car. He stood and returned to the office. "If Christine arrives after I've departed, please let her know the situation."

"Sure thing," she said.

He nodded, returned to the bench, and retrieved his luggage.

She watched him go, watched the taxi vanish into the distance. She kept her eyes on the horizon long enough that a negative of the landscape was burned into her eyelids when she closed them. She rubbed her eyes with the heels of her hands, blinked them until she could see normally again, and focused on her books.

The four day countdown began again.

That night, she held the panties in her hand like a security blanket while she slept. She woke a few times during the night with her fist near her face, breathing deeply, even though the most dominant scents were from her own hand. It helped her feel closer to Parrish, and she didn't want to let the panties go or just drop them in the hamper to be washed.

In the morning, she felt more than a little awkward waking up with someone's underwear in her hand. She hid them under her pillow to delay deciding what to do with them, then went to her office.

She didn't expect a call from Saul or Parrish explaining what had happened with the pick-up. Saul wouldn't see the need to update his hired pilot, and Parrish would have to find privacy to make the call or else risk explaining why she was sharing the information. She just told herself, once again, that it would probably wind up being a dumb, uninteresting story when she finally got all the details.

It was Friday, which meant ferrying a group of fishermen to Manitoba. She'd be plenty busy with clients and keeping her schedule straight, she wouldn't even have time to wonder about Parrish, Saul, or what might be waiting for her the next time she saw them.

She settled in behind her desk and got to work on her itinerary.

CHAPTER EIGHT

Tuesday

The plane was fueled up, washed, and ready to go. Garza had woken up early, dressed in her best outfit, and went to her office to wait for the already familiar growl of Saul's car. She'd gotten a haircut on Sunday night. Not to impress anyone, because it had been time. But she checked herself out in the mirror before she left the bathroom and smiled at her reflection. It wasn't a huge change, so she didn't expect Parrish to notice. But given how often she liked to grab handfuls of it, Garza hoped she at least noticed there was less to hold onto today.

Nine-thirty came and went, and the road outside the airport remained empty. She double-checked her watch against the wall clock to make sure it was running correctly, then went back to waiting. At ten, she went to tidy up the kitchen. She assumed Saul was sending her a message about punctuality, wasting her time the way she'd wasted his, something childish like that. It was stupid, but at least she could at least understand it.

She waited until noon, when it would be impossible to get him to Calgary before lunch even with the time difference, to call the number he'd left with her.

"Mr. Oakhill, this is Erika Garza out at Red Kite Aviation. I'm calling to remind you of the cancelation policy we discussed when you hired me. Lack of notice or failure to appear within three hours of the departure time constitutes a no-show, which I'm afraid means that you'll still be charged for today's flight. I'd be happy to fly you out tomorrow, if I'm available, but there's no guarantee I won't have another client by then. Feel free to give me a call back if you~"

She heard a car door shut and looked out the window, certain he'd arrived at the exact moment she'd looked away. She was incredibly surprised to see, instead of Saul, a Red Kite squad car. Two officers had gotten out. The driver was a cartoon cowboy, broad shoulders and a face that looked like it was carved from stone. His hair was a silver-gray blend that made him look distinguished, dependable. The passenger was shorter, barely coming up to his shoulder. She was Black and she was a little softer around the edges, but that just made her look trustworthy in a different way. He was Authority. She was Friend. It felt like a potentially dangerous combination.

"~if you, um, if you're still planning to travel tomorrow." She recited her number and then hung up, moving around her desk just as the officers reached the door and knocked.

"Afternoon," she said. "Can I help you?"

"Good afternoon." Even his voice sounded like a radio announcer, strong and steady with just a hint of southern twang. "Could I speak with E. Garza? It's my understanding he's the boss here?"

"I'm Erika Garza," she said.

He had the good grace to look abashed. "Apologies, ma'am, we only had the first initial to go with and made an assumption. I'm Sergeant Kyle Elver." He gestured at the woman. "Constable Shiela Rais. I was hoping you might help us answer a few questions."

"I... hope so," she said uncertainly. "Do you want to come inside?"

"That would be a big relief, thank you." He gave her a friendly smile as she stepped aside.

Rais nodded and said, "Ma'am," as she followed Elver inside. Erika closed the door and went to take her seat.

"So, uh, how can I help the Red Kite police?"

"Well, I'm afraid it's a bit of grisly business." Elver leaned forward, just a neighbor sharing some gossip. "We're investigating a suspicious death, and it seems as if you were the last to see the victim alive."

Garza was shaken. "What? Who?"

"Saul Preston Oakhill," Rais provided.

She almost asked 'what about him,' then realized what she was saying. She flinched and fell back against her chair, switching her attention to Elver again.

"You can't be serious."

"I suppose that confirms he was a passenger. We found your name and this address in his planner, but there was no real context for what it meant."

Garza nodded absently. "Yeah, he was a client. I f-flew him to Calgary and back again. Four times. Well, to Calgary twice and back twice." She rubbed the bridge of her nose. "I mean I took him there, and a few days later~"

"We follow," Elver assured her. "When was the last trip?"

"Today," Garza said. "Er, no, I mean, it was supposed to be today. I took him there Tuesdays and brought him home Thursdays. So the last trip would've been last Thursday."

Rais was taking notes. "These trips were over these past two weeks? Back to back?"

"That's right." Garza's brain caught up to her. "Wait, I can't be the last person who saw him alive. There was a taxi, he called a taxi to come pick him up."

Elver perked up at that. "Do you happen to recall the name of the company?"

"I don't," she said. "But he called from here. It would be in my phone records."

"You won't mind us looking those up?"

She shook her head. "No, go ahead."

Elver nodded his thanks.

A large portion of Garza's brain was dedicated to worrying about Parrish, if she was okay, if she had found the body, if they'd talked to her, before it connected to the main part of her brain.

"Wait, Parrish. Uh, Christine Parrish."

Elver and Rais both looked at her, waiting for context.

"She would've been the last person to see him alive. Right? Unless it happened right after he left the airport on Thursday."

"And who is Christine Parrish?"

"His partner."

A quick glance at his notebook, a page flipped, then flipped back. "We were told that was simply an employee at Red Kite National... there was no partner mentioned."

Garza shook her head. "No, I mean, she was... like his wife, but they weren't married. They lived together, though." That was right, wasn't it? She could've sworn one of them had said as much. "They were a couple."

Elver looked at Rais, who gave him a responding look that Garza couldn't translate.

"Ahh," Elver said, "all our evidence shows that Mr. Oakhill lives alone."

"That's... not right."

She tried to remember the explanation they gave. Work functions, parties, the appearance of normalcy...

"The people at his work would know. They've, she said they met her."

"No one we spoke to at Mr. Oakhill's bank mentioned anything about a wife."

"She's not his wife," Garza said.

Elver held up a hand in apology. "Partner. Regardless of what you call her, this is the first we're hearing of a 'Christine Parrish' in his life. Or any woman, in fact."

Her heart was pounding frantically. "I don't understand."

"How do you know this Miss Parrish?" Elver asked.

"She picked Saul up on Thursday. The first Thursday, anyway. And she was there when we made our arrangement." She took a deep breath and let it out. "I'm sorry. This is all very confusing. Can you tell me how he died? When he died?"

Another silent conversation passed between the sergeant and constable. "He was found last night by one of his neighbors. Coroner's report indicates he was dead for about twenty-four hours before that."

"What's suspicious about that?" she said.

Rais said, "The blunt force trauma to the back of his head."

Garza barely stopped herself from throwing up. "He was murdered?"

"Why did you think we're here talking to you?"

"I don't—" She put her elbows on the desk and covered her face with both hands. "I can't even process the fact he's dead. He was *murdered?* Who would want to murder him?"

"Nice guy?" Elver ventured.

"Not particularly," Garza said. "Kind of an asshole, honestly. But... a bland one. I can't imagine him making anyone angry enough they'd want to kill him."

"Maybe he had something they wanted."

Elver suggested it so casually that Garza almost didn't register it.

He had someone I wanted.

"Am I a suspect?"

The officers looked at her in unison. "Why would you be a suspect?" Elver asked.

"I don't know. You're here. Talking to me."

"You were the last person to see Mr. Oakhill alive," Elver said. "And you took him to Calgary twice, brought him home twice. That's as far as our interest here goes. For now."

Garza tried to ignore the ominous weight of the last two words. If she hadn't been a suspect before, she absolutely was now. Elver stood up, prompting Rais to do the same. Garza decided she should stand as well. He extended his hand.

"Thank you for your time, Miss Garza. We'll be in touch if we need anything else."

She picked up one of her business cards and handed it to him. "Any time. If I'm on a job, there's a messaging service I use."

"Thank you kindly," Elver said, pocketing the card.

She watched them go, waving as Elver did a three-point turn to get back to the road. As soon as they were off the property, she ran to her desk and picked up her phone.

She immediately put it back down. She'd just given the police permission to look at her phone records. It wouldn't look great if she frantically started calling Saul's number the second they left. She drummed the fingers of one hand on the desk, chewing the thumbnail of her other hand as she tried to think of what to do.

She couldn't take any flights. She'd cleared the afternoon to be with Parrish anyway, but she couldn't imagine being in the air if more news came in or if Parrish showed up to help explain what the hell was going on.

Saul was dead. Murdered. *Murdered.* And no one had ever heard of Parrish? How was that possible? But she suddenly realized that if anyone asked her for evidence the other woman existed, she wouldn't have anything to show them. A baseball manager who could be anywhere in the province now. That mechanic she flirted with in Edmonton? He would *definitely* remember her, but she couldn't even remember his fucking name now. Todd? Thomas? Travis? There was no physical evidence~

The panties.

She jumped up and ran through her house. Fear crept into her mind, dread that she would look and they'd have mysteriously vanished. She got to her bedroom, yanked back the blanket, and flipped the pillow over.

Parrish's panties were there.

Garza dropped heavily onto the mattress. She picked up the underwear and held it in both hands, staring down at the cotton like it was a holy talisman. She supposed, in a way, that was exactly what the panties had become. Proof she wasn't crazy. Proof that something bizarre was definitely going on, and Christine Parrish had been here. Was somewhere out there. For now, that was enough to keep her from climbing the walls.

And it freed her mind to worry about the actual mystery. Where the hell had she gone?

***

Sergeant Elver returned around four that afternoon. Garza tried not to look too eager, to desperate for information, but she felt like he wouldn't have come all the way out to the airport unless there'd been a sizeable development in the case. He looked apologetic when she opened the door but there was a hardness behind his eyes that told her this was all business.

"Sergeant," she said. "Tell me you tracked down Christine Parrish."

"Afraid not," he said. "We *did* confirm with the taxi company that Mr. Oakhill was picked up here and taken to his home. The driver didn't report seeing anyone waiting for him when he was dropped off. And we went ahead and spoke to Mr. Oakhill's neighbors. They're as baffled as we are. If we could get a description of her~"

She nodded. "Oh. Sure, uh. She's pretty distinctive. Australian accent. White-blonde hair~"

"Ah." He held up a hand. "Sorry. I didn't mean now. I'm actually here to ask if you'd mind coming down to the station with me. We have a few more questions we wanted to ask."

Garza frowned. "I can... uh, wh-why can't I just answer them now?"

"It would be better if we spoke at the station," he said. "Just for the formality of it."

Her breath caught in her throat. "What's... Why?"

"We found what we believe to be the murder weapon."

She watched his face. "What, it has my fingerprints on it or something?"

"It does." She blinked in surprise, but he kept going. "It also has something else."

She held her breath.

"Miss Garza, your name is literally written on it."

CHAPTER NINE

Tuesday, still

Garza sat in a small closet with a table, two chairs, a little table with a carafe of water and two glasses. She couldn't find a comfortable way to sit. Her hands kept shaking. Her right foot kept wanting to bounce. She felt positive Elver was doing this on purpose, making her stew and overthink and panic and worry. He'd barely said anything on the drive to town, going only so far as to be polite. But the message was clear: he wasn't a friend, and this wouldn't be a casual conversation like the first one they'd had in her office.

Elver finally came in. He was carrying a transparent plastic bag which he dropped heavily onto the table before taking his seat. Erika looked at it, immediately recognizing the wrench within. It was the one from her kitchen, the one she'd put on the table when Parrish suggested damaging the plane so she couldn't go get Saul. She couldn't remember if she'd put it away or not.

Most damning thing was the GARZA written in black marker on the handle.

"We found that in a ditch not far from Mr. Oakhill's home. I have to assume it belongs to you."

There was no point in denying it. "It looks like the one I keep in the kitchen."

"Have you ever visited his house, Miss Garza?"

She shook her head. "I don't even know where he lives."

"We asked a few of the neighbors about you as well," he said. "You've got quite a unique look, so we thought maybe someone would recognize you."

She looked at him, startled. "I was never there."

"No one remembers seeing you there," he confirmed, consulting a notepad. "But you claim someone was *living* there that the neighbors had also never seen. So maybe they're not the best witnesses."

Her panic cleared enough for one word, one idea, to manifest itself. "I think I want to call a lawyer now."

Elver nodded as if he'd been waiting for that. He reached into his pocket, took out a dime, and placed it on the counter. He left his finger on the coin so that when she went for it, he slid it back.

"I'm going to be upfront with you, Miss Garza. I would be very surprised if you did this. But you're being evasive. You're not telling me everything. That makes me nervous. And until I have those questions answered, I'm going to have to keep looking at you." He pushed the coin back toward her and stood up. "Come on, I'll show you where the phone is."

She took the dime and stood up.

Elver stood as well. As soon as he did, his expression twisted, like someone who had just realized he'd lost a chess match. "Ah hell."

Garza frowned. "What now?"

He held his hand flat above her head and moved it toward himself until it touched just below his chin. She raised her eyebrow at him.

"Mr. Oakhill was my height," he explained. "Give or take a little. That blunt force trauma I mentioned? On the back of his head?" He gestured to his own skull. "It was a downward blow. Unless he was sitting or kneeling, which the coroner doesn't believe based on how he fell after the blow, you couldn't have done it."

"So I can't be a murderer because I'm short?"

"Oh, I'm sure you're capable," Elver sighed, "but I highly doubt you did this one."

"You don't have to sound so disappointed."

He smiled, and suddenly he was the friendly uncle again. "I still have questions I need answered. If you still want a lawyer here..."

"I think it would be best."

He gestured for her to follow him out of the room.

The payphone was at the end of the hall, in a small wooden case that also included a phone book. She found the number for a lawyer - Anna Singh - and dialed. As it rang, she flipped through the book to the Cs, scanning the page. Paget, Painter, Park, Partridge... no Parrish. Flipping back to the Os, she almost immediately found Oakhill. She made a note of the address, just in case, as the phone was answered.

"Anna Singh and Associates, how can I help you?"

"Hi. I'm Erika Garza. I guess I need a lawyer."

Anna Singh arrived three minutes after Garza hung up the phone. She wore a dark red suit, her hair pulled back in a tight ponytail, and moved like she would smash through a wall if one happened to get in her way. Garza had gone into the main room to sit with Rais, and Singh spotted her immediately. She crossed the room to her seat, turning to speak to Rais.

"Where's Sergeant Elver?"

"His office." Rais started to rise. "I'll~"

"We'll be in the interrogation room. We're not to be disturbed." To Garza, she said, "Erika Garza? Anna Singh. Come with me."

Garza didn't believe it was a request, so she stood and followed. Singh held the door for her, then followed her inside and shut the door behind them.

"Tell me everything. Leave nothing out."

Garza said, "I've told them everything."

Singh shook her head. "Clearly not. I know Elver. If you told him everything, you wouldn't still be sitting here. So I need the whole story, including the parts you've been holding back because they're embarrassing or incriminating. I'm on your side, and everything you tell me is completely confidential." She sat down in the seat Sergeant Elver had previously used. "Start from the beginning."

Garza sat down. She scratched her head, then started to speak. She gave a description of meeting Oakhill and Parrish, then hesitated before going to the next part. She had to trust someone, and this woman had the power to get her out of the sergeant's crosshairs.

"That night, Christine Parrish came back to the airport and suggested an affair."

Singh looked up from her notebook. "She thought you were having an affair with Mr. Oakhill?"

Garza cleared her throat. "No, she... she wa-wanted, she... meant with me. She wanted to have an affair with me."

"Oh." She sat up straighter. "I see. How did you respond?"

Garza's face felt hot. "I... accepted."

Singh's face was completely unreadable. "Okay." She made a note. "Go on."

"You... you, uh, want details about–"

"That won't be necessary," Singh said. It was the first time Garza had seen her lose her composure. "So you and this Christine Parrish began a, um, physical affair. This continued into the following week?"

Garza nodded. "We were together while Saul was in Calgary. When he went back last week, Parrish spent those three days with me."

She continued to explain coming back with Saul and Parrish's failure to appear.

"Did anything happen that final day?"

Garza tapped her fingernail on the table, reluctant to get into declarations of love with this stranger.

"I'm beginning to see why Sergeant Elver is so frustrated by you."

Garza sighed and leaned back. "I told her I loved her. She didn't say it back, but she... I-I didn't need her to. It wasn't about that. I know how she feels about me. And... ah..." She ran her hand through her hair. "They have a wrench."

"A wrench?"

"It has my name written on it. It's mine, from my kitchen. I use it to work on the pipes when there's a problem. They found it near the crime scene."

"Do you have any idea how it got there?"

Garza chewed her bottom lip. "I gave it to Christine."

Singh raised an eyebrow.

"She made a joke about disabling my plane so I couldn't go get Saul. So we could have a few more hours together. I left it on the dinner table. I didn't notice it was gone when I came back because I never really think about it. It's probably been over a year since I used it."

"Okay," Singh marked something down.

"Elver said he doesn't believe I did it."

Singh didn't look up. "Then he probably means it. He doesn't lie just to trick suspects. But if he has questions, it's best to answer them. You, Miss Garza, presented him with a woman he doesn't believe exists and a wrench that may have been used as a murder weapon ending up at his crime scene. You are nothing but questions with no answers. And unless you're willing to tell him about your extracurriculars with this Christine Parrish, we'll have to find a way to settle his curiosity without giving everything away."

"I don't~"

"Don't worry about it," Singh interrupted. "That's what you're paying me for. Is there anything else you think I should know before I bring Elver back in here?"

"Christine Parrish exists. I can't prove it, but I know I didn't imagine her. I couldn't have just imagined anything about that woman."

Singh nodded. "Okay. I don't think we have to convince him of that, but I'll keep it in mind. Stay here."

She left the room and returned a moment later with Elver behind her. When she sat down, she took the other chair on Garza's side of the table. She faced the sergeant.

"I think we can wrap this up quickly and save my client some money. You have questions about the wrench, correct?"

Elver still hadn't finished sitting down. "Uh. Yes."

"Miss Garza confirms the wrench is her property, but she will state on the record that she hasn't used it in more than a year."

Garza said, "Oh. I don't know about... on the record..."

"To the best of her recollection," Singh corrected herself. "It could have been taken from her home at any time during that period and ended up being used for any manner of crimes."

"Someone broke into her house and the only thing they took was a wrench?"

"Are you certain that could never happen, Kyle? You've seen my client's house. Did you see any valuables that would have enticed a burglar? Maybe someone broke in, was frustrated by the lack of potential, and took something random just to make it worth his while."

He started to respond, then turned it into a sigh.

"I'd call that reasonable doubt," Singh said. "Now, as to your other point of interest that she's..." She checked her notes, then gave Elver a pitying look. "*Too* concerned about someone else's safety?"

"Someone we can't confirm even exists."

"Maybe she's private. Maybe she found Saul Oakhill with his brains bashed in, so she packed a bag and decided to take a vacation. Miss Garza is prepared to testify under oath that she met Christine Parrish on multiple occasions. Are you convinced we won't be able to track down *one* person who can confirm her existence?"

Elver leaned back in his chair.

Singh ran her eyes over the notepad. "You seriously had her bring me in for this? You should be ashamed, Kyle. Is this all you have? Can she go?"

Elver fixed his eyes on Garza, staring so hard she started to worry he could see her thoughts. She didn't know how to react to his attention, so she just stared back. She tried not to blink. Finally he sighed and looked away.

"Do you have a way to get home, Miss Garza?"

"I can take her," Singh said, checking her watch. "If I'm going to charge her for a whole hour, I can at least be useful."

Elver extended his hand to Garza. "I apologize if I caused you any undue stress."

She was so surprised by the apology that she almost forgot to shake his hand. "Consider it forgotten. I just... I-I want to know what happened."

"That makes two of us."

Singh escorted Garza out of the building to her car. The sun had gone down while she was inside and the street was full night, lit only by streetlights on either corner. Garza said she lived at the airport. Singh gave a nod and started driving.

"So that's it? I'm done with the police, no more surprise visits or being taken down there to be questioned in that little closet."

"You should be," Singh said. "If not, you call me again. Don't let them tell you no."

"I appreciate that. How much do I owe you for today?"

Singh said, "For *this?* I'm not charging you for slapping him on the wrist like that. He's a good guy, but he was abusing his power to satisfy his own curiosity. He should have just asked about the wrench and moved on. I don't mind doing that gratis. The woman who doesn't exist is weird. But I could tell he believed *you* believed she was real. If he thought you were just making something up off the top of your head, he would have gone after you harder. I think he believes you met *somebody*, it's just not clear *who*."

Garza finally relaxed into her seat. "Thank you."

Singh nodded, then said, "Ah shit. Wait. Buy me a coffee."

"What?"

"Do you have a dollar?"

Garza patted her pockets. She found some coins and counted them. "I have eighty-five cents."

Singh held out her hand, and Garza dumped the coins onto her palm. "Okay. I was officially employed as your lawyer for the past hour, so everything we talked about is covered by confidentiality. It's a formality but it will help you feel a little more secure that I won't blab about... anything."

"Oh. Thanks."

"Mm-hmm."

She pulled into the airport parking lot a few silent minutes later. She pulled up in front of the office and stared at the door for a long moment.

"There's a card game. First Thursday of the month. We alternate who hosts. It's me and a couple other ladies from town. Like-minded ladies." She looked at Garza. "If you're looking for something like that."

Garza was stuck on "couple other" ladies. She'd never imagined there was another gay woman in Red Kite, let alone enough for a card game.

"I'm... not really good at poker."

Singh laughed. "It's not really about the game. Sometimes we watch movies. Sometimes we just talk. You're more than welcome to join."

"Thank you. I appreciate that."

"Sure. The more the merrier."

Garza opened the car door, then stopped. "You've never met Christine Parrish, have you?"

"Describe her."

"Australian accent. White-blonde hair. About a head taller than me. Freckles."

Singh shook her head. "Doesn't ring a bell. And I think I'd remember the accent and the hair if nothing else. I'm sorry. Did you give that description to Sergeant Elver?"

She nodded.

"Okay. Then I'm sure he'll spread it around. If someone saw her, they'll speak up. And I'll ask the others, just in case they know her and aren't willing to admit it to the police for whatever reason."

"I appreciate that." She held out her hand. "Thank you. For everything."

"I'm happy I met you, Miss Garza," Singh said, shaking her hand.

"Erika."

"Anna."

Garza got out of the car and watched her leave, then went back inside.

Once the door was closed behind her, she was struck by a severe feeling of waking up from a surreal dream. She was supposed to have spent the past few hours naked and riding Parrish, not being driven into town by the police and questioned about a murder. Not being forced to out herself to a complete stranger. Not being asked to question her own sanity.

She hadn't realized how hungry she was until she turned on the kitchen light. She made a sandwich and ate it as she walked through the house to the bedroom. She flicked on the light and stared at the bed, trying to make sense of the past few hours. Whatever had gone wrong, it must have started on Thursday, when Parrish failed to show up. And there had to be a reason Parrish took the wrench with her when she left. It was a big, heavy thing, as long as her forearm, and it wasn't something that she could have accidentally carried off when she left the house.

There was something else that scared her. Elver said Saul had been killed by a downward blow. Parrish was taller than Garza, but she was shorter than Saul. Not by much, but enough that she would have to be stretching her arm over her head to deliver a downward blow, and Garza felt like that would take a lot of power from it. Would it still have been enough to kill with a hard enough weapon? Possibly.

The way she saw it, there were only two possibilities, and she didn't know which one scared her more. One, there was a chance that their conversation Thursday morning had made Parrish do something drastic, and now she was on the run or in hiding until she figured out what the next step might be. Or two, there was some third party out there who had killed Saul and Parrish was... collateral damage? A hostage? Was she in danger while the police were sitting around scratching their heads?

She went to her bed and sat down, staring at a random spot on the wall. She'd never even asked to go to Parrish's house instead of spending all their time at the airport. She tried to remember the brief interactions she'd seen between her and Saul. At the time, she'd been too jealous to pay close attention. Now that it actually mattered, she could only recall snippets. Parrish always seemed to be the one in charge. Saul telling her to stay in the car, but Parrish got out anyway. Parrish scolded him for being angry when Garza had been late and got him to apologize.

But what did that prove, except that she had some independence in the relationship? Garza knew that already. She didn't know what it meant, if anything, and she knew she'd drive herself crazy if she spent much more time twisting everything around trying to make it make sense.

She fell back onto the bed and closed her eyes, letting her brain rest, falling asleep with too many unanswerable questions swirling around in her brain.

CHAPTER TEN

Over the next two weeks, Garza took as many flights as possible. Long stretches to Winnipeg and Edmonton, a quick jaunt to Moose Jaw, an endless flight to Fort McMurray where an engine problem stranded her overnight. When she was home, she checked the newspaper religiously for any information about the Saul Oakhill case but, after the initial few articles, it was still unsolved and eventually the paper moved on.

She called Sergeant Elver three times to see if he had any information he could share. A suspect. A lead on Parrish. Anything. He had finally been forced to tell her to stop calling. "We'll let you know if we find out anything," he promised. "Consider it penance for coming down so hard on you when this all started. Deal?"

She reluctantly agreed.

The first Thursday of the month arrived. She didn't have any clients, and the idea of puttering around the airport would drive her insane. She needed to get away from the familiar and distract herself from worrying and building a list of questions that would just buzz around in her head like bees. She took out Anna Singh's card and chewed the end of a pencil as the line buzzed in her ear.

"Anna Singh Legal Services."

"Yeah, hi, it's Erika Garza," she said. "I was wondering if the invitation to tonight's card game was still available. You know, with the... with all your~"

Anna laughed. "Yes, I know which one you're referring to. You're more than welcome to join us, if you'd like. Let me give you the address."

She was excited about the party for a solid two hours, showered and did her hair and found an outfit that made her look cool and interesting - she hoped - and then went out to the hangar to get her bike. Then she thought about how her helmet would mess up her hair, and how noisy the bike would be in Anna's neighborhood, and they'd probably think it was annoying and she was annoying, and then the whole night would be awkward for everyone, so it was better if she just stayed home.

Then she pinched her earlobe and said, "Shut up, Garza, get your shit together."

Then she got on the bike and went to the party.

Her anxiety faded, for the most part, during the ride. By the time she arrived at the house, she felt almost like a functional human being.

Anna came out onto the porch. Her hair was down and she was wearing jeans and a flowy T-shirt, which made her look at least ninety percent softer and more approachable than she'd been at the police station. Despite Garza's fears, Anna was smiling like a kid on Christmas. She ran her eyes lovingly down the bike's length as she approached.

"You have a plane *and* a motorcycle? You might be the coolest person here."

"I'd be terrified if that was true," Garza said.

Anna laughed. "Come on in. The others are already here."

Garza followed her up the driveway. Three other women were waiting inside. Two women sitting together on the couch, both older, ("Carol and Amanda," Anna introduced) and another coming out of the kitchen with a bottle of Budweiser ("Marie"). The one with the bottle was Garza's age, with long brown hair and sharp features that came together to make her look solid and reliable. She gave a nod and raised two fingers in greeting when Anna said her name.

"And this is Erika Garza," Anna said, "pilot, biker, and occasional murder suspect."

"You said I was never really a suspect," Garza said.

Anna grinned and patted her on the shoulder. "Go with the story, kiddo. Makes me sound cooler for getting you out of the jam."

Garza laughed nervously. She noticed Marie seemed to be giving her a once-over, and didn't know if she was sizing up a threat or preparing an attack.

"Everything set up?" Anna asked. Marie nodded, so Anna motioned for everyone to move into the kitchen. "All right, Erika's first game is ready to go. No one take it easy on her. I represented her pro bono so I'm looking forward to taking some cash from her tonight."

Marie lingered so she could walk into the kitchen with Garza. "So you're a pilot?"

"Yeah, that's right."

Marie nodded. "That's pretty cool. I'll have to convince you to take me up sometime. I'll repay you with a tour of the fire station."

"You're a firefighter?"

"The only one in town," Marie said. "Everyone else is volunteers. I keep the wheels turning."

"Oh. That's cool," Garza said. "And yeah, we could... we could trade. Sounds fun."

Marie took a drink, winked at Garza with the bottle still against her lips, and went to take her seat. Garza, against her better urges, took the opportunity to check out Marie's ass. It was a very nice ass, and the jeans seemed to have been made specifically for her curves. A very nice sight, and worth taking the trip into town all on its own.

Anna was shuffling a deck of cards and started dealing. "So, Erika, you gonna join us or are you just going to stare at Marie's ass all night?"

The other women laughed as Garza blushed, but Marie just smiled. "Cool, so it worked." She winked at Garza again as she took one of the chairs around the dinner table. Garza sat across from her.

"So it's usually just the four of you?" Garza said. "Can you play poker with just four people?"

"Sure. Sometimes we have guests." Anna dealt. "Marie will be dating someone, or Carol's sister will be in town. And when your friend shows up again, she'll be more than welcome to join us." To the others, she explained, "Erika's got a friend who is missing."

Marie tilted her head to the side. "Murder charge, you're a pilot, and now a mystery about a missing person? You're the most interesting person we've had in years."

"She also has a motorcycle," Anna said.

The women made a sound of amazement.

Marie said, "I hope we're not making light of something serious."

"It... might be. I don't know. I hope not..."

Anna sensed the discomfort. "We don't have to talk about that right now." She moved a few chips to the center of the table. "But if any of you know her friend. Christine Parrish?"

"Australian accent," Garza said, feeling like she was reciting from a card. "White-blonde hair. Freckles."

They all shook their heads sadly as they placed the antes. She could see they were trying their best to place the mystery woman so Garza waved it off as if it didn't matter.

"It was a long shot anyway. Tonight's supposed to be about distracting myself from all of that." She picked up the cards Anna had dealt her. "You're going to have to explain some things to me first. Most of these cards just have faces and letters on them. A, K, Q, J, how can I tell how good they are? And should they all be the same color like this?"

Carol and Amanda folded.

Marie grinned. "You're dangerous, fly girl."

Garza shrugged. "If you want to take a fool's money, go ahead and stay in."

Anna chuckled. "Oh, you are going to be fun."

As soon as Garza let go of the mystery of Christine Parrish for the night, she ended up having a great time. Carol was hilarious, a woman in her sixties who had only come out of the closet six years earlier when she and her best friend finally admitted their feelings for each other. Amanda, Anna, and Marie were all deeply closeted, but they'd found each other through various dating escapades and encounters at bars in Saskatoon and its surroundings.

"It's rough out there," Anna said, "reading signals and trying to find the one other lesbian in the province you and your friends haven't already dated."

"Who knew there was one hiding out at the airport?" Marie said, taking a slow drag off her cigarette, keeping her eyes on Garza.

Garza blushed.

She ended up winning two dollars which, given what they were betting, was a fortune. She was helping Anna clean up when Marie motioned her aside.

"I liked meeting you tonight," Marie said.

"Oh! Yeah, it's a great group."

Marie smiled. "Yeah. I'd kind of like to not wait until next month to see you again. If that's all right."

"Oh, like taking that flight you were talking about?"

"Sure," Marie said, chuckling softly. "Or maybe a movie. There's a drive-in two towns over where we could go."

It took her a second to realize she was being asked on a date. "Oh! Really?"

She almost told the truth, that she really didn't go to the movies. Or maybe it was too soon after everything with Parrish... if this period of time really *was* 'after Parrish', which she wasn't sure she was willing to admit. But Marie was beautiful. And funny. And it didn't have to be anything more than two new friends getting to know each other.

"I don't have a car. Just the bike."

"That's fine. I can pick you up."

They exchanged phone numbers and tentatively agreed the movie would happen on Sunday, unless Garza was booked for a job.

On the ride home, she kept turning Marie's number over in her mind. She expected she'd have it memorized by their movie date.

Their date.

Her first real date in... who knew how long? No, that wasn't true. Could she count the trip with Parrish as a date? She assumed so. They'd gone to a game, had dinner, slept together. That was a date by anyone's metrics. But Saul had made it feel different. There was no real endpoint with Parrish, no expectation that maybe one day they'd truly be together. Or as together as the law would allow.

With Marie, there was hope. A chance that it could be more, that she would be the only other person in the relationship.

She didn't want to give up on Parrish. Not yet. But the longer she was gone, the easier it was to see beyond her, to take off the lust-colored glasses and see reality.

Waiting for Christine Parrish was a quick route to heartbreak. Maybe it was time to see what the rest of the world had to offer.

The movie was *Raiders of the Lost Ark*. The opening scene was exciting enough, but Garza couldn't stop thinking about the woman sitting next to her. The drive-in offered a strange kind of public privacy. The car made them relatively anonymous, so they could make out if they wanted. But there were cars on either side of them and either of the people in those cars could glance over and realize they were seeing two women kissing.

Of course every time Garza glanced over, she saw that any potential witnesses were too preoccupied to notice anything outside their own cars.

Marie didn't push things either way. She just sat and ate her popcorn, sipped her soda, and watched the movie. Eventually Garza forced herself to focus on the screen.

"I'm having a hard time following this," she said. "Are you confused?"

"No," Marie said. "But I've seen it before. And I've been looking at the screen instead of running around inside my brain."

Garza flinched. "Sorry about that."

"Don't be. I know we joked around at poker night, but you're going through a hell of a time. The woman you've been sleeping with vanishes the same time her husband gets killed? I'd be going insane. If you want to consider tonight just a, you know, pause button on everything, that's fine with me. I'm happy to provide that. And it's a pretty fun movie."

"Yeah, seems like it. I liked that guy in the space movie."

Marie smiled, nodding. "And Marion is pretty hot, too."

Garza chuckled. "Yeah."

"Looks kind of like you."

"We should have parked closer to the screen if your eyes are that bad."

Marie snickered and sipped her soda. "She must have been really special, hm? Christine?"

Garza started to answer, then stopped and put her thoughts in order. "It was just supposed to be sex. Fun, no strings attached, killing time while her husband was out of town. She called them ghost days. Like Christmas and your birthday. Special days that feel different than ordinary days, you know?" Marie nodded that she understood. "We only had six days together total. I know it's crazy to think we've made a real connection in that time. Or maybe it's not. But those days... they felt like more by the end. And having that taken away... it hurt."

"I understand," Marie said. "And look, six days or six years. The honeymoon period can be a hell of a drug. But when you know something, you just know. There's got to be something special about this Parrish woman if she's still got this tight of a hold on you."

Garza said, "You think?"

"Erika, you're sitting in a car with a sexy-as-hell firefighter who is willing to let you do whatever you want in this region." She gestured to her torso and lap. "And you haven't made the first move. So either you've got something else on your mind or I'm about to get very self-conscious."

Garza laughed and looked down at her hands. "It's definitely not you."

Marie nodded. "Okay. Well, you take as long as you need. And I'll be here, either as a friend or..." She shrugged. "Or for whatever you need me to be."

"Thank you. That means a lot."

"You're welcome." She pointed at the movie screen. "There's a really good gag coming up..."

Garza settled in. She wasn't fully relaxed, and her mind was still turning Parrish's name over and over again, wearing smooth the edges of it. But Marie's words had helped calm the storm a little bit. It gave her hope that maybe someday, maybe someday soon, she could forget about Parrish and move on.

It was enough for her to relax and enjoy a movie with a beautiful firefighter.

CHAPTER ELEVEN

Garza returned from a marathon trip to Vancouver on a Wednesday night. She had to stop in Calgary to refuel, which gave her flashbacks to the trips with Saul. It was almost exactly a month since Christine Parrish first walked into her life. Two weeks with her, two without. And when the 'without' period started with an unreturned declaration of life and a murder, she felt like moving on was the only viable path.

Maybe with Marie. Marie was pretty. She was fun and smart. And, when they realized neither of them could focus very much on the movie, she had proven herself to be a fantastic comedian. Garza had laughed more at her than at the movie. She could see herself dating Marie. It would be easy. Well, as easy as a relationship like theirs would ever be.

She landed, put the plane to bed, and headed inside. She would call Marie in the morning. They'd make plans. Maybe just a quiet dinner at one of their houses. She was excited at the possibility.

Garza had eaten dinner in Calgary so she passed through the kitchen and went straight to her bedroom. She untucked her shirt and started undoing the buttons as she turned on the lights.

Parrish raised both her hands as if warding off an attack. "Please don't scream."

Garza thought it was more likely she'd throw a punch. She couldn't classify any of the emotions she was feeling in the moment. Relief, joy, anger, confusion, frustration, panic, fear. It was Parrish, but her hair was red now. She was dressed in a man's white undershirt and blue jeans. It would have been a good look for her, but the clothes were dirty, as if she'd been wearing them for days. Her hands, still raised in defense, were shaking.

Garza stepped closer, like she was approaching a potentially feral dog. She reached out and brushed her fingers down Parrish's cheek. Parrish closed her eyes and leaned into the caress.

"You're real," Garza said, breathing a sigh of relief.

Parrish opened her eyes again. "What? Of course I'm real. Why-"

The kiss was like an attack, and Parrish actually flinched away from it before she realized the intention. Garza pushed her back against the wall, forcing Parrish's mouth open with her tongue, arms around her waist like she was afraid of falling or being pulled off of her. Parrish returned the kiss with equal passion once she got her footing, holding just as tightly to Garza.

They parted to breathe, but kept their faces close to each other. Parrish's breath was bad, and she smelled of sweat and grease, but at the moment Garza didn't care.

"When was the last time you took a bath?"

"I don't remember." Parrish's voice broke.

Garza stepped away from her. She slipped her hand into Parrish's. "Come on."

She drew a bath while Parrish took off her dirty clothes. She paused before taking off the underwear.

"I don't have anything else-"

"You can borrow mine," Garza said. "Something has to fit you."

"Thank you."

Garza stepped away from the tub, looking down so she wouldn't be distracted by her nudity. Parrish sighed as she settled into the water. She drew her knees up to her chest and wrapped her arms around them. She looked so small and frightened that any anger Garza felt was quickly overwhelmed by her other emotions. She sat on the floor next to the tub.

"So. Where the fuck have you been?"

Parrish whimpered and put her hands over her face. "Quebec."

Garza was sure she'd heard wrong. "Jesus. That's... far."

"Yeah." She laughed and a tear rolled down her cheek. "Probably should've flown. Know any pilots who could've taken me?"

"So. What happened?"

Parrish wiped at her eyes and muttered something under her breath. "I'm sorry I just vanished. I was scared. I wanted to come see you but I had to leave as fast as I could."

"Don't worry about me. What happened to Saul?"

"I don't care. I came here first. Let him worry."

Garza tensed. "Wait. You don't know?"

Parrish stared at her.

"Christine. Saul is dead."

Parrish's face went paler. "What? What do you mean?"

"Someone bashed his brains in. With *my* wrench. The police thought maybe I did it for a while."

Parrish stared at the water, eyes darting back and forth. "No," she whispered. "I didn't do it. I'm sure I didn't."

Garza put her hand on Parrish's arms. "Did you take my wrench?"

"Yes," Parrish said. "I-I was... I was..." She pushed her hair out of her face. It still looked shocking with color. "I didn't think, I just picked it up, and I thought, I thought I'd wait for him to get home and I could hit him with it, and then we could be together. But I didn't do it. I know I didn't. Because halfway home I looked at it and I saw your name written on the handle and I knew the police would find it and they'd think you did it and I... I..." She furrowed her brow, thinking hard. "I think I threw it out the window."

"You're positive you didn't go home before you got rid of it?"

Parrish kept staring. "No."

Garza got on her knees and moved closer, leaning over the edge of the tub. "Christine. Why did you have to leave town so quickly?"

"Because they were coming."

Garza narrowed her eyes. "Who, baby?"

"Saul is really dead?"

"Yeah," Garza said softly. She stroked Parrish's hair. "I need you to focus. I need to know what the hell is going on here."

Parrish sniffled. She still had the thousand-yard stare, and she was trembling, but the color had come back to her cheeks. She licked her lips and reached up to grip Garza's wrist.

"We told you Saul is a banker. And that's true. He, he, he takes care of people's finances. He's good at it, but he was terrible at getting clients. People don't like his personality. So he was struggling. And then one day a couple of guys come in and make him an offer. They wanted him to be their personal banker. They paid him really well for anonymity and privacy because their income isn't... strictly legal."

"He was laundering money for criminals."

"And brokering deals for them. His personality works really well for that. He doesn't get emotional, so he never comes across as stressed or anxious. He's like a robot from a science-fiction movie. So he does really well in negotiations."

Garza moved her hand to Parrish's shoulder and squeezed.

"The Calgary deal... it wasn't... he was..." She looked at Garza, then past her into the hallway. "Are we safe here?"

"Yeah. We'll be fine."

A shudder passed through Parrish. Garza reached for the shelf and took down a washcloth. She wet it, then started rubbing Parrish's arms. "Turn around. Face that way for me."

Parrish turned in the tub, facing the wall so Garza couldn't see her face.

"I asked people about you. The police asked people about you. Saul's neighbors had never seen you. No one had even *heard* of you. How is that possible?"

"Because *I'm* his neighbor," Parrish said with a soft laugh. "They probably knocked on everyone's door and asked if they had ever seen a woman living with him. And there was one house where they didn't get an answer. That's because it's my house. Saul bought it for me. He wants me in his space as little as possible. But I have to be close enough to pop in if one of the people he works for shows up. So there's a gate in the backyard. If he turns on the porch light, I head over and play the good wife for however long he needs."

"And sometimes you sleep over?"

Parrish shrugged. "I'm still attracted to him. I want to be with him, even if..." She put her head down on her knees. "Before I met you, being with him was the only physical affection I had. I couldn't go out and meet anyone."

"And the people at work?"

"They went to his legitimate work. The bank. He didn't have to pretend there because he didn't care what they thought of him. I was strictly for the criminals, so they'd think he was one of them." She sniffled and rubbed her hand under her nose. "He didn't want to give them anything they could use as blackmail."

Garza swept the towel down Parrish's back. "So that's why no one in town had ever heard of you."

"Why would they have? I didn't exist. Never went out. Didn't even have to go to work anymore." She looked over her shoulder. "I was a bank teller, by the way. I guess I either didn't make much of an impression or there's been enough turnover since I left that there was no overlap. That's how I met Saul. Tall, handsome man who dressed well and didn't take part in the typical boy's club bullshit. He was polite and considerate. Anyone would've fallen for him. I thought I was special when he chose me. I guess we just looked good together."

Now that she seemed a little less shell-shocked, Garza tried again. "What happened the day you vanished?"

Parrish tensed. "I went home. I didn't have the wrench with me when I went into the house. I remember now. My hands were free. I thought about the wonderful things you'd told me. I thought about what I would say to Saul when he got home. I really... I-I thought he might understand. He's not my warden. If I told him I wanted to spend more time out here with you, he would've understood. Maybe."

She sighed and turned around to face Garza.

"There were people in his house. I saw the car when I went home, and I thought, 'who would be visiting him now?' So I went to look in the car, see if I could figure out who it belonged to. That's when one of them came outside and saw me. Saul warned me. He said if anyone ever showed up looking for him, I should run. So I did. I just ran. I'm fast, but the guy who came out was faster. He grabbed me. I fought, but he was too strong.

"The other guy came out. The guy who grabbed me said they could use me as a bargaining chip for whatever they wanted from Saul. I ended up in some building. They tied my hands and asked me when Saul would be back. I told them." Her hand flew to her mouth. "Oh, God. I got him killed..."

Garza said, "No. Saul got himself killed. Whatever he was doing for those guys got him killed. You just kept yourself safe." She brushed Parrish's hair out of her face. "What happened next?"

Parrish thought. Garza briefly entertained the possibility she was making this all up as she went along, but it felt authentic. It felt more like she was remembering events that she'd blocked for being too traumatic.

"They left. They went to wait for him at the house, and they left me alone. I guess they thought I'd just sit there and wait for them to come back like a good girl." She huffed a laugh at that.

Garza smiled. "You showed 'em, huh?"

"They were shit at tying knots. I managed to wriggle free in just a few minutes. I thought about coming here. Honestly, I did. But I couldn't bear the thought of bringing you into all this. So I followed the train tracks until I got to the station and I just bought a ticket. I only got off at Quebec because it felt like it was far enough away. People were speaking French. It felt like a different country. Like I might be safe there."

"And that's where you've been the last two weeks?"

Parrish nodded. "I found an underground poker game and won enough money to get a room, some clothes. Get my hair done." She flicked her hand toward her hair. "Enough for a disguise. I tried to think of where to go next. I just wanted to be safe. Forget about everything back here and start over somewhere." She looked at Garza. "I couldn't do it. I had to come back."

"Those men killed Saul," Garza said. "If they find out you're back, they might come after you to take care of any witnesses. You got away, you should've stayed away."

"But you were here."

Garza blinked, taken aback. "I'm... I'm not worth~"

Parrish kissed her. She rose up out of the water, sitting on her knees now, and cupped the back of Garza's head, moaning softly when Garza finally gave in and returned the kiss.

"I love you, too," Parrish said against Garza's mouth. She was breathing hard, her breath still bad but now Garza was beyond caring. "I was three thousand miles away from the people who had thrown me in the backseat of my own car and left me tied up in an abandoned building and all I could think about was how I hadn't said that to you. I would've regretted it for the rest of my life if I didn't. I had to come back, Erika. I love you."

Garza swallowed the lump in her throat. "Finish your bath. Brush your teeth. We'll go to bed and sleep on it, a-and I think we'll both think a lot clearer in the morning."

"Can I have something to eat before bed? I'm starved."

"Yeah, I'll see what I can find."

"Thank you."

Garza kissed her. "Thank you for coming back. I missed you."

Parrish sniffled and nodded.

"I'm going to go make you something to eat."

"Okay."

Garza managed to keep her stride normal and her legs steady until she was in the kitchen. As soon as she was positive Parrish couldn't see her, she reached for the wall to brace herself just as her knees gave out. She'd given up hope. She'd been positive she would never see Parrish again, that she was gone for good. And then the relief of having her back had been twisted by the truth of why she'd left. The danger that was still out there.

Shaking, she carefully made her way to the dinner table and sat down. She squeezed one hand into a fist and closed the other hand around it. She focused on a spot directly across from her. She pretended she was on a plane. The engine was out. She was drifting. Coasting toward a rocky coastline, and she had only seconds to decide whether she should try a rough landing or risk going in the water.

She closed her eyes.

She made her choice.

CHAPTER TWELVE

Monday

She didn't know which one of them instigated the sex. It could have been Parrish, unable to sleep and climbing on top of her. But Garza had been thinking about it when she fell sleep. Maybe she was the one who reached out, who rolled her body until she was pressed against warm bare skin. She only knew that her first conscious thought was a weight on her and Parrish's hands slipping around her waist. Her lips responded automatically, body rising up off the bed as Parrish settled onto her, pinning her down.

"Tell me I'm real again," Parrish whispered.

"You're real," Garza said, happy to remind herself again. She flicked her tongue out to taste whatever part of Parrish it happened to touch.

"What's my name?

"Christine Parrish."

She sobbed quietly. "I felt like nobody. I was free and safe but I... and even... with Saul... he didn't see me as a person. I forgot. I forgot I was a real person until you said you wanted me, Erika. Until you saw me. You saw me and you knew I was real, oh my god."

"You're Christine Parrish, you're real, and I love you." Garza kissed her hungrily, pulling her down onto her.

Parrish settled between Garza's legs and thrust with her whole body, grinding down onto her with enough force that they both grunted.

"I'm real," Parrish said. "And I want you."

"I want you too," Garza whispered, then sat up and slid her lips across Parrish's cheek to her ear. "I want you." She understood what that meant now, how much Parrish needed to hear it. "I want you so much. You're all I want, Christine."

Parrish put her head down on Garza's shoulder and thrust harder against her. When Garza clung tighter, Parrish turned the grunting into words.

"I love you, I love you... I love you..."

Garza closed her eyes and held on as tightly as she could.

***

She woke alone the next morning, but she refused to let herself panic. She put on a robe and went into the kitchen to find Parrish sitting at the table with a cup of coffee in front of her. It didn't look like she had actually had any of the coffee, but her hands formed a protective bracket on either side of the mug. She was wearing one of Garza's T-shirts and a baggy pair of shorts.

Parrish jumped when Garza entered her periphery, closing her eyes as she relaxed. "Sorry."

"I think you have a reason to be jumpy." Garza sat down. "How are you doing?"

"Heh, ooh. I don't know." She looked down at her coffee. "I've never been here on a Monday. It's weird. It's like being in school on the weekend. Or maybe it feels weird for... for other reasons."

Garza said, "Yeah. It's kind of weird having you here like this for me, too." She bit her bottom lip and looked down at the table. "I gave up, you know?"

Parrish looked at her.

"On you. Coming back. Seeing you again. I thought... okay. That was all I get, that's fine. And now all of a sudden you're back. It's like whiplash. I feel like I'm all twisted around. I'm happy you're here. I'm *so thrilled* that you're here, don't get me wrong about that, okay? I just need some time to get my feet back under me, you know?"

"I understand."

Garza held out her hand. Parrish took it. "I want you here," Garza said.

Parrish squeezed her hand. "You do?"

"I do. And I wanted to say it when we weren't naked and doing stuff to each other so you know I mean it." Garza stood up and kissed Parrish's forehead, then her cheek. "I'm going to make us some breakfast."

"Okay."

She went to the fridge and, thankfully, found that she had enough for two breakfasts. She remembered going grocery shopping with Parrish their first week together. She hadn't thought much of it at the time, but Parrish had kept to herself, clung to Garza's side like a toddler, never venturing too far from the cart. Now she realized she had actually been hiding. She looked back at the table, where Parrish was staring into her coffee.

"I'm sorry you had to live like that."

Parrish looked up at her. "It was my choice. I thought that was the only way I could get what I wanted. And I guess I just thought that eventually I would wear him down. Or convince him he wanted me." She laughed softly and shook her head. "Stupid."

"Hopeful," Garza said.

"Means the same thing, right?"

"Not if you hope with the right person."

Parrish raised her eyes again. "I thought I had to fight and work for what I wanted. I didn't think anyone would just... be willing to... just... give it to me."

"Love does take work. Relationships take a lot of work. But it's not a one-person job."

Parrish stood up and went to join Garza in the kitchen. "What can I do to help?"

Garza grinned. "I didn't mean literally, right now. I can handle breakfast. But you can get the plates and silverware if you want."

"Plates and silverware. On it."

Garza finished cooking and they carried their food to the table.

"You don't have to have an answer now," Garza said when they started eating, "but do you know... I mean... what the hell you're going to do next? You're more than welcome to stay here as long as you want. But if the guys who killed Saul are still out there I don't know if that's the safest choice. The police looked into me. Even took me to the station for questioning~"

"Oh my god I'm so~"

"I don't care about that. It's not about that. I just mean if these criminals have connections, they might find out. They might come to see why I was connected to Saul's murder at all. So I think it's good to have a plan. What do *you* want to do?"

"I don't know," Parrish said. "Honestly I don't have a single clue. If they went so far as to actually kill him, something must have gone *really* wrong. Maybe they were just tying up loose ends. Maybe... maybe they're long gone."

"They know you're still out there somewhere. You're a loose end."

"But they might not think I'm worth chasing after, right? As far as they know, I'm just the wife. They wouldn't risk getting caught just to hunt me down. And even if they did, they wouldn't expect me to still be this close to town."

Garza considered that and decided it might be true. She was about to respond when Parrish suddenly tensed, her eyes focused on the window behind Garza.

"Do you have any clients today?"

Garza turned. A car was heading toward the airport. It was too far away for the driver to see in the house, but close enough that Garza recognized it as Sergeant Elver's patrol car.

"Go. Hide in the bedroom."

Parrish stood. "Erika..."

"Go! Shut the door. Don't make a sound."

"I'll turn myself in," Parrish said. "It'll end this all for you, it'll be over. You shouldn't have to deal with any of this."

"Maybe I don't want it to be over if that means losing you." Garza cupped Parrish's face and kissed her. "You're worth it. Now hide."

Parrish left, and Garza realized she was only wearing her robe. She swore, cinched the belt tighter, and tried her best to make sure she wasn't revealing too much. The car stopped just in front of the kitchen door and Elver unfolded from behind the wheel. He scanned the horizon, let his gaze linger on the plane, then strolled up to the door. Mr. Casual, Calm, and Cool.

Garza answered before he could knock, and he smiled. "Were you expecting me?"

"Benefit of having a really long driveway," Garza said, pointing at the road.

Elver twisted at the waist as if he hadn't considered it. "That would make it pretty hard to sneak up on you, I bet."

She didn't know how to take that comment, so she just let it go. "How can I help you, Sergeant?"

"Well, you were still sounding pretty shaken up last time we spoke. Constable Rais pointed out that you might not be as, um, accustomed to death as we are. And even we still get pretty rattled from time to time. Especially when it's a bad one like Mr. Oakhill. So I just wanted to be sure you were doing okay, processing things well."

"Oh. Uh. I appreciate that. Really. And I've-I've been... doing okay."

"Sleeping well?"

She nodded. "Yeah, pretty much."

"Good, good." He nodded and his eyes drifted. "Two plates."

Garza didn't understand the context. She followed his eyeline until she saw the dinner table. Two breakfast plates. Two cups of coffee. She slowly faced him again.

"I'm not sure what my personal life has to do with anything."

"No," he said, looking toward the plane again.

Or.

Maybe.

He was looking for a vehicle for her overnight guest.

She cleared her throat. "Well. So yeah, um, I'm doing okay. I'm sorry I've been bothering y'all so much, it's just that, you know, it's not something I'm used to. Like you said. It's very shocking. No one I've known has ever been murdered before."

"We found Christine Parrish."

Garza wanted to throw up, gasp, and fold into herself all at the same time. She was frozen in place, which she was grateful for, because it kept her from sprinting into the bedroom to make sure she was still there.

"You did."

"Her bank account, at least," Elver clarified, steely eyes locked on her. "Same bank where Mr. Oakhill works. And from there we were able to get her address. You're never going to believe this, but she lives right next door to him. Little fence in the backyard connecting the two properties. It's a nice little arrangement."

Garza said, "Oh. I'm glad that all got sorted out."

He smiled. "Yeah, same. Same. Especially since for so long it felt like no one knew she existed. I mean *no one*." He chuckled and shook his head. "You, though. You knew her."

"Yeah. Like I said, she showed up with Saul. Drove him home."

"Mm-hmm. That's right. You mentioned that."

Garza crossed her arms. "Is something wrong, Sergeant?"

"No," he said, letting the word ride out on a sigh. "Nothing you need to worry about. But I've got a dead man here and no killer, a ghost woman that apparently only you have ever seen, and both of them have bank accounts that would make Scrooge McDuck go blind. Now, that definitely gives me a motive, which is nice. But it doesn't get me any closer to actually locking anyone up for it. You're a weird piece of the puzzle, Miss Garza. I like you. And I don't think you're misleading me, or pretending to be anything you're not, but you *are* keeping something from me. I don't want you to sic Anna Singh on me again, but I'm asking you. Unofficially. Help me out here."

"I can't," Garza said softly.

Before Elver could make another appeal, a voice came from behind her. "Have you looked at his client list at the bank?"

Garza tensed, frozen in spot, wondering if there was a way she could pretend she'd spoken instead. Elver furrowed his brow and leaned to the side, peeking past the doorframe so he could see Parrish as well. She was standing in the doorway leading to the rest of the house. She'd put on Erika's pants with one of her light tan shirts tucked into it. Elver looked at Garza, a disappointed appraisal, and then he finally nodded.

"We looked at the clients in his ledger, yes."

"There's a second ledger," Parrish said. "In his house. There's a floor register between the living room and the kitchen. For the heater." Elver nodded. "There's a second ledger there with the real names and figures."

"We didn't find that," Elver admitted. "Miss… Parrish, I presume?"

Parrish nodded, eyes on the floor. "That's right."

Garza dropped her head in defeat. "Christine, what the hell have you done…"

"Stopping you from going to jail for lying to protect me."

"So *you* go to jail instead?"

Elver held up his hands. "Hold on. No one is going to jail here. In fact, I was preparing to offer Miss Garza immunity for information. Miss Parrish, if you truly had nothing to do with Mr. Oakhill's murder, I'm willing to extend that same offer to you. We're looking for murderers here. Whatever financial crimes you, Miss Garza, and Mr. Oakhill may have been involved in, I'm sure we can find a way around it."

"Erika isn't involved in any crimes," Parrish said. "She's totally innocent in all of this."

"Then…" He looked between them. "You said you only met a few times. But you're withholding information from the police to protect her, she's hiding out in your house, you're having breakfast together, she… she seems to be wearing your clothes. Why would you go to these lengths for a woman you claim to have only met in passing?"

Garza looked at Parrish, who didn't seem eager to reveal this particular secret. Elver watched Garza, then seemed to finally notice her robe, even though she'd said she had seen him coming. She tensed as she watched him do the math in his head, probably adding in the fact that Saul and Parrish had separate finances and lived in different houses.

"Oh," he said.

"We're not doing anything illegal," Garza said meekly.

Elver swallowed hard. The surprise in his face prevented her from reading any other emotions, disgust or understanding, either direction would have told her where they stood.

"This answers your questions, right?"

"I suppose." His voice was strained. He lifted his hand to point at Parrish. "I'd like to have a, ah, more thorough conversation with you, Miss Parrish. But for the time being, I'm going to... head back to Mr. Oakhill's house and check out that vent you mentioned. I'll be back. You'll be staying here, I assume."

"For as long as she needs to," Garza said.

Elver nodded. "Okay. Well... okay."

Parrish stepped forward. "I'd like to go with you, actually. I'm going to need to pack a bag from my place if I'm going to stay here. And I think it would be a lot safer going with a police officer."

Garza said, "It would go faster if I helped."

He sighed. "Fine. Go... go dress."

Garza went to Parrish and took her hand, guiding her into the bedroom. As soon as they were out of Elver's line of sight, she turned and grabbed her shoulders.

"What the hell were you thinking?"

"I couldn't let him go on suspecting you. I appreciate what you were doing for me, but I couldn't just stand there and hide when I~"

Garza kissed her. "I love you."

"I love you, too."

"When we get through this, we're going to sit down and figure some stuff out. Okay?"

Parrish nodded. "Yeah."

"For now, we should hurry. I don't think Elver's going to wait too long for us to get ready."

CHAPTER THIRTEEN

Monday, still

They rode to Saul's house in the backseat of Elver's patrol car. Garza truly believed he was on their side, but she couldn't shake the feeling that they were being taken into custody for coming out to him. She and Parrish sat far enough apart that they could have fit another person between them without touching, but she still felt conspicuous when they got into town.

During the drive from the airport, Elver had used the radio to ask Rais to pass by Oakhill's house to make sure the coast was clear. They were a few blocks away when she radioed back.

"Nice and quiet out here, Kyle. Need me to stick around?"

"Not necessary," he said. "I'm coming up the street right behind you."

"Well, hey there." She gave a wave out the window as they passed. "Did you pick up a couple of troublemakers?"

Elver tried to cover a smile as he glanced at them in the rearview. "No, they've been behaving. I'm just playing taxi today."

"Always nice to serve a purpose," she laughed. "Bring lunch when you come back."

"From Cady's?"

"Where else is there?"

Elver chuckled and hung up the microphone. He parked in front of Saul's house and turned to face them in the backseat.

"I'll take you in your place first, Miss Parrish. Have a look around and make sure the coast is clear. Once I'm satisfied I'll head over to Mr. Oakhill's. Sound like a plan?"

They agreed.

Elver led the way across the yard, one hand on his belt near the holstered revolver. He knocked on Parrish's door, waited, then motioned for her to unlock it.

"I don't have the keys." He looked at her, incredulous. "I didn't think, I just ran. I don't think I even locked the door when I left."

Elver looked at the door. He tried the knob and it turned easily in his hand. He sighed, shook his head, and held up a finger to tell them to wait while he went ahead.

Once he was inside, Parrish took Garza's hand. Garza squeezed.

"It's gonna be okay."

"I know," Parrish said. "As long as you're here, I can believe that. I'm just reminding myself that you're right here."

"And not going anywhere."

Elver came back. "Okay. Coast is clear. But be quick about it. Just pack the essentials and come find me next door. Understood?"

They agreed and went into the house. It was the first time Garza had been in Parrish's personal space, and she took a moment to appreciate it.

The living room was cozy, messy in a lived-in way. A sweater tossed over the back of a chair, magazines and newspapers left out. She saw a stack of romance novels tucked away almost out of sight next to the couch and hid a smile, hoping she could take a couple of them when they left. They would need reading material if they were going to be hiding out for the foreseeable future, after all.

Parrish went directly to the bedroom. Garza followed the sound of drawers opening and closing. A bag was open on the bed. Parrish was taking clothes from drawers and tossing them in, turning away without making sure they landed properly.

"You're going to need all of this?"

"No. Maybe. I don't know. He probably won't let us come back here, so I'm just... I'm taking whatever I can grab."

"Let's just be calm and rational, okay? No need to weigh ourselves down with outfits for every occasion."

Parrish took a breath. "I'm scared."

"I know you are. That's why I'm here. Come on, let's pack a real bag."

She chose a few summer outfits, and a couple of heavier things in case Parrish's exile extended into winter.

Parrish was forced to determine they had enough when Elver called to them from the front yard.

"Ladies, will you come out here for a moment?"

As they passed through the house, Garza detoured and grabbed a few romance novels off the top of the stack by the couch. Parrish saw her stuffing them into the bag and her cheeks went pink.

"Those are just~"

"Oh I know what they are," Garza said. "And I look forward to reading some of them with you. Getting ideas."

Parrish smiled.

They joined Elver on the front lawn. He was holding a ledger and he used it to gesture toward the horizon. "Would you read the words on that hill for me?"

Parrish looked, but Garza kept her eyes on Elver, confused. "Hills...?" she said, knowing full well the land was flat for hundreds of miles in any direction.

"Yeah," Elver said. "Nice green hill, big white letters on it. Can you read what it says?"

"There are no hills," Parrish said hesitantly.

Elver leaned forward as if trying to look through a mirage. "Oh yeah. Huh. Must mean we're not in Hollywood. And *this* is not a movie. You're going to sit tight and let the police deal with this." He held up the ledger. "These are bad men. They're not James Bond villains but, Miss Parrish, you know very well what they're capable of. We're equipped to handle men like this. Let us do our jobs. Okay?"

"We will," Garza said.

He watched her for a moment longer than necessary, as if waiting for her to flinch, then nodded. "Okay. Have you got everything you need?"

Parrish held up the bag. "Yes, sir."

"Okay. Let me drive you back to the airport."

On the drive back, they sat closer together in the backseat. Garza had the bag on her lap and her right hand on the seat between them. Parrish slid her hand across the seat and slipped her fingers around Garza's, then tightened her grip. He may suspect something improper between them, after catching them half-naked having breakfast together. And he didn't seem to have an issue with it, other than vague discomfort, but the less evidence they supplied, the better.

"There is... one more thing," Elver said once they crossed the town limits. He sounded reluctant, flexing his fingers on the steering wheel before he spoke again. "The money in your bank account, Miss Parrish. It's a pretty hefty sum."

"Yes," she said.

"According to records, you deposited all of it yourself. All cash transactions. No transfers from Mr. Oakhill's account. Which means we have no way of knowing where exactly that money came from. And I have no legal reason to press you to tell me where it came from. Or... hell." He sighed and looked out the window. "Maybe I do. Who the hell knows. The point is, I have no interest in pursuing that line of inquiry. Do you understand what I'm saying?"

"I do," she said. "Thank you."

"Don't thank me," Elver said. "Just making you aware of the situation."

Parrish smiled. "Well, then thank you for the information."

Garza cleared her throat. "So do you think there's actually a chance you'll find these guys?"

Elver met her eye in the mirror. "Honestly, I think having you bunker down is an abundance of caution. I thumbed through the book and I recognized some of the names. These guys, ah, they're financial crooks. They got in over their head when they murdered Oakhill and they probably rabbited. Like I said. Not a movie, not James Bond. We'll track them down and then you can get back to your normal lives."

"Whatever that looks like," Parrish muttered.

Garza looked at her. Her whole adult life had been built around Saul, waiting for him to summon her, waiting to be paraded around like a prop. It had gotten her a home, but at the expense of a life. Parrish turned to meet her gaze and smiled, squeezed her hand.

Maybe after all this mess, they could both end up with something good.

"She bit back a scream as the rogue pressed her against the tree. She barely reached his chest, which she could see through the shirt she'd torn as she ran from him. Though she tried with all her might to wriggle free, he pressed his body against hers, and she felt his desire hard and thick against her stomach even through all the clothes between them."

Garza struggled to keep her face neutral as she closed the book on her thumb to look at the cover models, then looked at Parrish. They were lying together in bed, Garza in pajama bottoms and a T-shirt and, for the first time, Parrish was wearing one of her own nightgowns. It made her look softer, frailer somehow. She was curled against Garza's side, and what she'd intended to be titillating had, instead, turned into something more like a bedtime story.

But the content...

"You... you like this stuff?"

Parrish laughed. "I know it's not great literature. Or even good writing, for that matter. But that's not what I read them for."

Garza kissed the top of Parrish's head. "It turns you on?"

"Well, yeah," she said, squirming closer. She brushed her hand over Garza's stomach. "It just has to be good enough to give you the mental images. And... sometimes..." She bit her lip and chuckled softly, then shook her head. "Never mind."

"No, say it."

Parrish looked at her, searching her face, clearly having a mental debate about whether or not to say what she'd been planning to say. Finally she gave a defeated sigh and shook her head.

"Sometimes... the way it's written... not this one. Hold on."

She got out of bed, making Garza regret her question. Parrish crouched next to the bag and searched until she found another book. She brought it to bed and handed it to Garza as she reclaimed her position, wiggling until she found the warm spot she'd just abandoned. Garza looked at the cover, which seemed almost identical to the previous book. Sexy muscular man, chest exposed, pants tight enough to hint at his attributes. One muscular arm wrapped around a small woman's waist as she bent away from him with a look of terror on her face.

"This looks like a crime," Garza said.

"In real life, sure. These guys would be locked up for sure. But that's not what the books are *about*. They're about fantasies and giving in and... and..." She hunched her shoulders. "Sometimes I would pretend I was the man in the scene."

Suddenly Garza was interested. "Oh really."

"The way some of them are written, the sex scenes are from the man's point of view, and I don't know, I started imagining it was me. And I was aggressively going after these sexy women."

"Kind of the way you walked in here and came after me that first night."

Parrish laughed softly and pressed her face against Garza's shoulder. "God, that was so much fun. And so terrifying. I thought maybe... given how you were dressed and your swagger, and the way you looked at me. I thought, if anyone is going to react right to this, it's her. It took every ounce of courage I had, but I did it. When you told me to leave, I felt like such an absolute fool. Like a little kid playing dress-up and being sent to my room."

"Wow. I didn't get that at all. It felt like you were *very* in control."

"I knew what I wanted. And I'm so glad I took the risk and went for it."

"Me too." Garza flipped open the book. "So you imagined you had a throbbing shaft that you wanted to sheath in her willing..." She raised her eyebrows. "They can publish that word...?"

"Oh they can publish all kinds of things," Parrish said. "But they like tiptoeing around the really harsh stuff as much as possible. They make you work for it. I like 'shaft.' And 'sheath' is good." She took the book back from Garza and flipped through it. "Here. This one. *He gazed down into her wide open eyes, his passion almost painful inside his trousers. He took her hand and guided it to his desire. Her small fingers traced the length of it and her eyes widened further, her mouth forming a wide oh, wide enough to...*" She cleared her throat and squirmed.

"Should I leave you three alone?"

"Absolutely not." Parrish rolled over on top of Garza. "You will not escape my clutches. I will have you tonight before anyone else defiles your honor."

Garza laughed but let herself be pinned. "These authors should be in prison."

Parrish grinned and rose up over her. "Perhaps I should give that whippish tongue of yours something else to keep it occupied..."

"There's got to be better smut in the world," Garza said as she sunk down into the mattress under Parrish's overwhelming attack.

But, for now, she was willing to explore Parrish's interests and see where it went.

Something cracked. Garza tensed as she woke up, her head lifting off the pillow. Parrish hadn't woken up, and Garza remained as still as possible to avoid disturbing her just in case it turned out to be nothing. She listened closely and another sound came. It was a quiet squeak, prolonged, like someone prying nails out of wood. She wasn't ready to panic, but she knew it was more than just the house settling on the foundation.

Their pre-bed activities had left her sore. Parrish had played the man, using her fingers and being as rough as Garza allowed her to be. It had been thrilling to look up and see Parrish thrusting against her, breasts swaying, hair covering her face, lips parted in what was almost a predatory sneer. She had become an animal, and it had been incredibly arousing to watch her truly let go.

But now it was Garza's turn to be the predator. She slipped out of bed, checked to make sure Parrish remained asleep, and pulled on her pajama pants and a shirt. There were more sounds coming from the outer room now, and she could pinpoint it to the office. She didn't have any weapons. The best option was sitting in an evidence room at the Red Kite police department. When she passed through the kitchen, she took a knife from the chopping board and held it low by her side.

She paused at the threshold to the office. The security light by the runway was on, and that shone brightly enough through the windows that she could see one man standing by the desk while a second was still halfway through the window they'd wedged away from its frame. She stepped forward and smacked the light switch, filling the room with light that she hoped would startle the intruders into dropping their weapons.

The man who was still halfway through the window swore, lost his balance, and fell back to the outside. The other man threw his hand up to block his face, holding the other up in what would've been a submissive pose if it wasn't for the gun it held.

"Hold on, sweetheart."

"Bad opening," she said. "Get out."

The other man was making another attempt to get in through the window. The first man said, "We don't want to hurt you. In fact, hurting you goes *against* what we're trying to do. We need you in one piece so you can help us."

"You have a funny way of asking for help, buddy. Hey!" She pointed the knife at the second man, who was once again straddling the sill. "Go the other way. I'm not kidding."

The first man said, "We're not exactly in a position to go through normal channels, so we had to resort to extreme measures. We'll be happy to pay the cost of the window once everything is said and done here. But we're in a real bind and we could use your help."

"Not interested. I'll pay to have my own window fixed, thanks."

The gunman sighed. "Look, we got off on the wrong foot here. Let's start over. Friendly-like. My name is Loomis. The guy squatting in your window is March. And we know you, you're Erika Garza. You're the pilot here. As it turns out, we have need of a pilot. See, your friend Sergeant Elver has eyes all over the county looking for us. Ain't nowhere we can go around here without someone dropping a line and letting him know which way we're going. But if we can start a hundred, hundred fifty miles from here, well, we might have a real chance of making our great escape. You get me?"

"And you expect me to fly you."

"Not even for free. Paid very well. Very, very well. We just have to get out of town. We stuck around too long trying to get our hands on money that piece of..." He stopped himself, becoming aware of how fried his voice had become. "We missed our window to get out before the net fell. This is our only way to slip off without making a fuss."

Garza was very aware that these were probably the men who had kidnapped Parrish and tied her up, keeping her prisoner. If she hadn't escaped, she doubted they would have come back with such a friendly offer of partnership. And if they found out she was in the house... March finally managed to get all the way inside the building and was checking his suit for tears.

"How much money are we talking here?"

"A thousand bucks. Cash on the barrelhead, free and clear. Plus whatever the cost for the window is. We're real sorry about that, but we couldn't just come knocking in the middle of the night."

"It might have helped the whole 'we just want help' angle. That, and losing the gun."

Loomis shrugged. "We're criminals, Miss Garza. We have to take precautions. Get the upper hand. That's the secret to negotiating, you know. Start strong."

Garza considered taking the offer, getting them into the plane and away from the airport as quickly as possible.

"Where do you think I'm taking you?"

"We've got some loose ends to tie up in Calgary. Sally caused a real fucking mess there when he tried screwing us, so we need to deal with that before we move on. But that won't be your problem. You get us that far and we'll be out of your hair and you'll have a nice stack of bills in your pocket when you fly back here."

"Don't listen to them, Erika."

Garza's shoulders slumped. "Seriously?" she said under her breath. "You're going to do this *twice* in the same day?"

Parrish came out of the hall. She was still in her nightgown, hair mussed with sleep, but her eyes were clear and focused. To Garza's surprise, she also had a gun, and it was aimed directly at Loomis' head.

"Christine, what..."

"They'll kill you the second you land the plane. They keep saying they'll pay you cash. Where is it? Stuffed in their coat pockets?"

"It's out in the car. We were going to go get it once we settled on the price." Loomis smiled. "Lovely to see you again, Mrs. Oakhill."

"That's not my name, Andrew. I never married Saul."

He shrugged as if the distinction didn't matter to him. "Well, whatever your name is, it's a *lovely* coincidence to find you here. We thought we'd have to give up on ever closing the book on you. The hair is a nice touch, by the way. Never liked the ice queen look. But now things have gotten very interesting." He raised his gun and leveled it at Parrish. "Because this bitch is hoarding money that's rightfully ours, and fate has led us right to her."

"If that's what it takes to end this," Parrish said, "you can have the goddamned money."

Loomis narrowed his eyes. "Forgive me if that sounds a little too good to be true, darling."

"I'm dead serious. Here's the deal. You want Erika to fly you out of here? Fine. She'll do it. You'll pay her appropriately. And in exchange for letting her leave Calgary alive, you get everything in the bank account Saul set up for me. Every red dime."

"That's a fortune," Loomis said. "And you'd just give it up?"

"Don't underestimate the price of having you out of my life forever, Andrew." She gestured with the gun. "It's a simple deal. Once Erika drops you off and radios that she's back in the air safe and sound, I'll contact the bank manager. It's late, but he'll take my call. He had a little crush on me when I worked there. I'll arrange to have the money transferred anywhere you choose first thing in the morning. You can give the info to Erika, that way she'll have to get back to the plane safely or you get nothing."

Loomis looked at March. He shrugged. "It's a good deal. And it's one less body to deal with."

"What's to keep her from backing out once the pilot is back in the air?"

"Because as long as she's alive, I don't give a shit about the money," Parrish said. "It's worth it to keep her alive."

"Who the hell is she to you?"

"She's my rogue," Parrish said.

Despite the circumstances, Garza couldn't help but smile a little at that. Loomis looked between them, trying to figure out what he was missing, but then he gestured with the gun and shook his head.

"Fine. Whatever. We'll walk away with most of what we want in the end. Miss Pilot, you can go get changed. We'll wait." He looked at Parrish with something almost like respect. "But I have to admit, I wish I had half an idea who the hell you really are, lady."

Garza looked at Parrish as she passed by her to go get dressed. "I wouldn't mind getting an answer to that question myself..."

CHAPTER FOURTEEN

Before

Christine sat with her legs tucked under her, reading one of her romance novels. She was biting her lip, her fingers teasing the collar of her shirt. She fanned herself a little and widened her eyes as she pictured what she was reading, squeezing her thighs together, wanting to touch herself but not daring to. Not yet. She knew the *really* steamy scene was still ahead and she wanted to wait for it.

Christine smiled and handed the deposit slip to the customer, shirt buttoned to her throat, round glasses perched perfectly on the bridge of her nose. "Thank you for banking with us," she said for the tenth time that day, the hundredth time that month, the millionth time in her life. Sometimes she wondered how many more times she would have to say it. "I can take the next customer, please."

Saul P. Oakhill stepped forward. With his long face, his deep voice, perfectly tailored suits. His long tapered fingers lightly holding the pen as she signed the withdrawal form. She had noticed him before, oh yes. She was very familiar with his well-tailored suits and quiet demeanor. Those steely eyes...! She had always fantasized about him coming up to her window with an invitation to dinner. Unfortunately today he only had a deposit slip.

"Well, hello, sir." Maybe he wanted to do a little roleplay. Pretend they were strangers. That could be fun. She processed his deposit while he waited silently, hands folded on the counter. She placed the money in the drawer and handed back a receipt. "Always nice to see you," she said, hoping her voice sounded steady.

He looked confused, as if he didn't know how to respond. Then he nodded, and walked back to his desk without saying anything.

She watched him go, full of longing.

***

Christine dreamed of Saul in her books. But he wasn't always the hero. Sometimes *she* was the hero, a knight or a duke, some mysterious royal who was used to getting what she wanted, and sometimes she tore Saul's clothes off and had her way with him. She woke from those dreams sweaty and desperate, her clothes usually twisted and pulled out of place. She wanted him to take her and she wanted to be taken by him, but she also wanted to be the taker.

She slipped a pillow between her thighs and rubbed against it until she could get some relief and fall back to sleep.

"I have a proposition for you."

Saul's voice was businesslike, serious and sincere, and she nodded eagerly. "Anything."

He finally met her eye.

"It's a bit unusual."

She leaned forward with interest.

In her mind it was a steady progression of A to B to C. She didn't think about the long stretches between their dates, or how long it took him to finally propose to her. Well, technically. She only remembered that it sounded like a wonderful deal. She would get her own house, for free. She would get paid a stipend for her service, enough that she could quit the bank and do whatever she wanted with her days. And she could be with Saul.

"When you say we'd be a couple," she said, testing the waters one night when they were alone in his car. She kept her eye on the road ahead, the twin cones of light from his headlights. "Do you mean... well, I'm just saying that people who have been intimate tend to have a certain, um... a certain... well, you know, an intimacy."

He tensed slightly in his seat, hands tightening on the wheel. "You're suggesting we go to bed together. In my experience that isn't the sort of thing a man should assume with a woman who, despite public performance, is merely an acquaintance. Is that something you would desire?"

"Yes!" She realized how eager she sounded, and she ducked her chin, touching the rim of her glasses in an attempt to hide her face. "I-I mean. I find you attractive is all. I wouldn't have agreed to do this if I didn't."

Saul considered it. "I suppose that would be acceptable."

It was hardly an enthusiastic yes, but that night he escorted her into his bedroom. He undressed for her, let her touch him and do whatever she wanted. He made the right noises, creating a soundtrack she'd only imagined when she read her books. She touched him and watched how his body responded to her, amazed to see it in real life, to be creating such a reaction. He was like an amazing, wonderful toy, and she couldn't imagine ever getting tired of playing with him.

***

But even the extraordinary can become routine, given enough time. Getting everything you want can become boring when fantasy turns into reality. Saul didn't live up to her fantasies, but that was fine. She still had her books. She still had her pillow and her fingers when he didn't get her where she needed to go. But she went with it because it was the life she'd been given. No one liked the life they were given, and most of them had to worry about where they'd live or how they'd pay their bills. She didn't have to think about any of that stuff. It was better. And it wasn't like there was anything better out there she was missing out on.

The first lie she'd told was that she and Saul had a mutual agreement about their relationship. She knew and accepted the activities he got up to on his business trips. But she'd let Erika believe she did the same thing here at home when he was gone. That would involve going out. It would involve meeting people. And she wasn't really interested in going to bed with random men. She didn't want sex just to have sex, she wanted it to mean something. And that would require being vulnerable. It was easier to stay home and live vicariously through her books.

Then she saw Erika Garza.

Saul brought her along with him because he needed her to know where the airport was so she could pick him up after the Calgary trips. It was one of his minor but horrible traits. She could just look at a damn map, but he wanted to show her himself. It was condescending, infantilizing bullshit, but she was accustomed to it by now, so she went along with it.

When she first saw Erika, she thought she was a man. Petite, sure, but she liked smaller men. Even from a distance, she could tell the person would be shorter than her. So she made the decision to get out of the car – which was quite hot, to be honest – and go get a closer look. It wasn't until she was almost on them before she realized she was looking at a woman. A beautiful woman with short hair and a strong frame and eyes so brown they were almost black.

And she realized there were possibilities out there beyond Saul.

Things she'd never considered, ideas she'd never let herself have. Not even when she was reading her books, imagining herself with a cock and tearing dresses off beautiful women.

She watched Erika carefully while she spoke with Saul. Listened to her voice, the rough timbre of it and the rasp at the back of her throat. She could be manly. She could be masculine. But she was definitely feminine. There was a duality, a blend of the two, that Christine found intoxicating.

She couldn't stop thinking about it on the ride home. Saul tried speaking to her twice, but she barely heard anything he said. It was a wonder she was able to respond to anything he said.

"What did you think of the pilot?"

Christine whipped her head around to look at him. "Why?"

"Merely curious. You seemed to have a fascination."

"No," she said, probably too quickly. "She was just... unique. That's all."

Saul made a noise in his throat that meant he acknowledged what she said but had nothing to add to the conversation.

When she got home, she opened the bottom drawer of her nightstand where she kept her naughty magazines. She sat on the edge of her mattress and flipped through them for anyone who looked anything like the pilot. Some had similar builds, but they were blonde or their breasts were far too big and obviously fake. Their hair was always long. No one had a short boyish cut like Erika's.

Christine flipped the pages with more urgency, running her eyes across butts, bushes, breasts, and none of them gave her even a twinge of what she'd felt while looking at the fully-clothed pilot.

"Fuck," she whispered, slapping the magazine shut and tossing it onto the floor.

She knew she could go to Saul. It would be far from the first time she'd fantasized about someone else while they grappled. But those had been men, celebrities she'd seen in a movie. It felt wrong doing it with a woman. And with someone she theoretically could actually be with. If she wanted. She'd seen the way Erika looked at her. There had been want. Desire. Hunger. Christine was confident that if she asked, the answer would be yes.

She shuddered at the thought. Her nipples were hard, and there was a humming between her legs that she felt the urge to deal with. But she wouldn't. She would see Erika again in a few days. Saul would be gone. And she'd have three whole days to explore these new urges.

She bit her lip and went to the bathroom to take a long, very cold shower.

On the day she dropped Saul off at Red Kite Aviation the first time, she drove away just far enough that he wouldn't see the car. She pulled off to the side of the road and watched, waiting, until finally she saw the plane soaring into the sky. She drove back to the airport and left a note in the doorway. She wanted Erika to meet her at the bar in town, a bar she'd never been to but somewhere she could consider neutral territory for what was sure to be an interesting conversation.

Erika wouldn't be back for four hours. Four whole hours before she even saw the card. Stupid. Why had she given herself so much time to sit and wait and think of all the ways it could go wrong?

She decided to use the time to prepare. She was not going to be timid. She wasn't going to be scared Christine, nervous Christine, the virginal lesbian asking the sexy pilot to please kiss her. No. She was going to be confident. She would be like the rogues in her romance novels. She was going to demand what she wanted. Maybe if she faked aggression, Erika would be more likely to give in.

Christine told herself not to cry when she came.

She bit her knuckle, squeezed her eyes shut, moved her hips against Erika's mouth, and angrily admonished herself for even thinking about crying.

But oh god it felt so good...

She was covered in sweat and her thighs were sore, her toes curled so tightly that she had to focus to straighten them. Her body was twitching in strange ways that she didn't understand, like she was recoiling from imaginary touches, hyper-aware of Erika's lips and tongue on her skin as she kissed her way up her body.

"You all right?" Erika whispered against Christine's mouth.

"Uh-huh," Christine managed, closing her lips around Erika's bottom lip, turning it into a kiss. She put her arms around Erika's neck and held her tight. It felt like days ago when she'd told Erika to "do whatever you want to me," and Erika had definitely taken that directive and run with it. She was still shaking, and she held tighter to Erika in an attempt to hide it. Erika sat up and there was just enough light to see the outline of her face.

"We're not done, right?" Christine asked, stroking her hand down Erika's back, looking up at her in the darkness. "We... Is that it?"

"Doesn't have to be," Erika said, breathing heavily. "Are you tired?"

"No," Christine said, even though she was, because she knew sleeping would mean the night would be over. "I want to do that again. Or something like that."

Erika grinned and moved her hand down Christine's side. "I can think of a few things like that you might enjoy."

"Show me," Christine said.

Erika moved her hand between them, and Christine closed her eyes, hoping she could survive three days with this woman.

They put on a show when Christine picked Saul up from the airport. Of course, she and Saul put on a show of their own. He called her "my lady," and Christine had jumped into his arms to give him a crushing hug. But she couldn't resist looking at Erika when she did it, licking her lips suggestively as Saul held her. He took the car keys from her and she settled into the passenger seat, watching Erika as he drove her away from the airport.

Away from Erika, away from the beautiful life she'd gotten a glimpse of the life she could have. Back to a quiet house. Romance novels and empty beds.

"Is something wrong?" Saul asked once they were on the road. "You seem distracted."

"No," she said. "Sorry. Um, how was your trip?"

"Uneventful outside of the official purpose. Mr. Loomis will be pleased with the progress we've already made, but it will require more negotiations, as expected. I hope you won't mind being without me for another few days next week."

Christine tried not to sound over-eager. "It's what we planned." She looked at the airport receding in the side mirror. "I'll find something to keep me occupied."

Maybe, on a normal weekend, she would have noticed something going on with Saul. In retrospect, if she'd known he would be murdered for trying to con the people who hired him, she would have picked up on some behavior that might have acted as a warning. But he honestly could have caught fire during those four days and she might not have noticed. Everything reminded her of Erika. A song on the radio, seeing a shirt she'd worn at the airport draped over the edge of the hamper, taking a shower and remembering the bath...

They had dinner together on Saturday night, sitting across from each other in Saul's dining room. He had a book open next to his plate and ate slowly, methodically, sometimes finishing a page before he took a bite. Christine didn't know why they had to be together for these weekly dinners. He claimed it was bonding, to make them appear comfortable with each other when they went out. But after spending so much time with someone who actually enjoyed her company, she couldn't help feeling like Saul saw her as a pet.

"Saul," she said.

He looked up, waiting. She tried to think of the right way to phrase her question. She didn't want to blow up a good thing, not even for Erika. What they had was so new, so different, that she couldn't predict if the ground would fall out from under their feet in a few more weeks. But she needed to know if there was a line he refused to cross.

"The men you meet up with on your business trips…"

He tensed and closed his book on a napkin. "We don't have to discuss that."

"No, I think we need to," she said. "I think it's important to know going forward. What happens if you… if there's someone you meet there that you have actual feelings for?"

"It's not a circumstance worth considering," he said carefully, "because there is no future there."

"Of course not, I'm not talking about marriage and white picket fences. I'm talking about more than… this." She gestured at the dark living room. "Coming home to someone who cares about you. Having dinner with someone who enjoys your company even if you're just sitting there reading a book. Wouldn't that be better than just having some hired actress pretending to be your wife?"

He frowned. "Are you worried I no longer enjoy your company? Christine, you are very adequate company. I find you charming. You're beautiful. I'm fortunate to have you as my partner."

"But I'm not your partner. And I think… *you* deserve better than just playing house."

Saul looked down at his food for a long moment as he gathered his thoughts. "The encounters I have when away on business," he said carefully, "are not relationships. It would be foolish to consider them such. They're trysts. There's no point in hoping for more, expecting more, because that sort of partnership is illegal. In Canada, in the United States, everywhere I can consider worth living. So I enjoy what I have, when I have it. The men I choose to spend that time with understand it as well. And if I happen to spend time with a man more than once, he knows it's merely because I enjoy his company and not an expectation of more."

"So it's not even worth hoping for."

He stared at her. He stood up and walked around the table to crouch next to her chair. "I'm not hoping for that, Christine. I'm not interested in changing anything about our arrangement. I don't know why you're suddenly so worried about that, but I can assure you I'm not going anywhere." He took her hand and brought it to his lips, kissing the knuckles. "I do care for you very much."

She looked at her hand in his. It was sweet of him to think she was asking the questions because she was worried about being left behind. It proved he cared. Maybe that was enough. Maybe she could *make it* be enough. Especially if she had Erika in her life. Saul was right. It was foolish to expect anything different, anything better, anything solid. White picket fences. She would never have that with Saul, but at least they could go out in public together. She would never be able to tell people she was with Erika, that they were partners. They would have to come up with lies and cover stories to explain their life together and keep the truth a closely guarded secret.

She was never going to happy. So she might as well stay in the unhappy secret that let her live a comfortable life.

"Can I stay here tonight?"

Saul looked surprised, but then he nodded. "Yes. I think that would be nice."

She bent down and kissed him. She hadn't had much experience with kissing before going into this relationship, and kissing him had always been fine. But now she had Erika to compare it to...

She wouldn't be stupid. She wouldn't risk everything for a possibility, for a second secret life that kept her hidden away.

This was as good as she could expect, and she was going to force herself to be happy with it.

And then Erika had to go and fuck it all up.

"I love you."

No one had ever said those words to her. Not even one of her parents, not a boyfriend, definitely not Saul. And here was Erika, whispering it in the dark, probably thinking Christine was asleep and unable to hear it. Saying it not because she had to, or because she was trying to get something in return, because she wanted to say it. Because she felt it. Christine's favorite person in the world had just said "I love you" and Christine knew she felt the same.

"Erika?" she whispered after some time had passed. Erika's body rose and fell with a deeper breath, but she didn't react to her name being said. "Erika?" Christine said, a little louder, still no response. Christine watched the line of her shoulder as it rose and fell like the tide washing in on shore. Steady and predictable, sleeping with her, pressed against her, both of them naked, stinking of sweat and sex.

"I love you too," Christine whispered, and she knew she was ready to blow everything up for this woman, for this new thing they'd found. Maybe it would end up being the worst decision of her life, but she'd been living with so many bad decisions for so long, and this one felt almost like, possibly, hope.

She didn't know how she was going to do it. And she was certain she'd overthink things in the morning. But for now, she had made her decision.

If she had to live a secret life, she was going to make it a life she was proud of.

And then...
And then...
All hell broke loose.

She was prepared. After Erika left for Calgary, Christine drove home planning to do whatever needed to be done to get the life she wanted rather than the one she was stuck in. She stole the wrench from Erika's house, but she'd never planned to use it. Or maybe she had? Just as a threat? To show Saul she meant business? But she never would have actually hurt him. He wasn't a bad man. He would have seen reason and let her go. That was why she'd thrown it out the window, wanting to erase that brief moment of insanity before she let it into her home.

And then.

She had seen the car parked in Saul's driveway when she got home. Its very presence was confusing. No one ever came over to see Saul, especially not in the middle of a workday. She parked at her house and crossed his lawn to peek in the car windows, to see if she could tell who it belonged to. She was almost to the car when something crashed inside Saul's house. She almost ran then, maybe could have made a clean getaway, but the front door swung open and a man stormed out.

They locked eyes and she saw his face change. He gave her the least sincere smile she'd ever seen and lifted his hand in greeting.

"Hey. Oh, hey. You're the wife, right...? We just want~"

She ran, but he was faster. He called for his partner as he wrestled with her, getting her arms pinned to her sides. Together they had managed to wrestle her into the backseat of their car.

"What the hell we gonna do with her?" the second man asked, out of breath.

"Bargaining chip," the first one said. "Oakhill's going to be a lot more willing to talk if we're keeping the missus somewhere."

They gagged her, tied up her hands. Then they drove her to that awful place.

She didn't want to think about the rest of that afternoon. They hadn't hurt her any more than necessary, hadn't done anything unseemly. But just the fact of being held prisoner in a filthy abandoned building felt like she was facing her judgement. Like the whole ordeal had nothing to do with Saul, but was instead a punishment for thinking improper thoughts, for wanting something sinful and illegal. She had taken out a pair of scissors, she'd opened them around her puppet strings, and suddenly the universe smacked her in the face.

When she got free, she just ran. No plan. No safety net. The universe had sent her a message and she'd received it loud and clear.

You are Bad and Wrong for wanting this, and if you pursue it again, you will not be as fortunate. This was a Warning.

She knew she would never be able to stay away from Erika if she stayed in Red Kite.

So instead she tried to find out how far she could run before her legs gave out.

She made it three thousand miles before the pain was too much. Before missing her became too awful. She couldn't sleep. When Tuesday rolled around, she felt a physical ache being away from the airport. *I should be with her. I should be kissing her right now.* She sobbed and stayed in bed all day, in the shitty little hotel she'd found.

But still she tried to run. She knew alcoholics went through this same thing when they decided to stop drinking, so she told herself she just needed distance.

She dyed her hair red. Erika had never seen her with red hair, so she wouldn't recognize her. She would be a stranger if they passed on the street. One more lane of distance between them.

It still wasn't enough.

She dreamed of Erika.

She craved her touch.

In Quebec, facing the choice between continuing her flight into America or finding a way to Europe, she looked at her reflection in a dirty bar mirror and surrendered.

I have to go home, she told herself.

Home was Erika Garza.

And she was going to do whatever the fuck she had to do to get there and stay there.

Chapter Fifteen

Now

Loomis spoke as soon as Garza came back into the office. "There's been a change of plans."

Garza finished tucking her shirt into her pants. "Oh, good. I was hoping for a monkey wrench in this meticulous plan you geniuses have concocted."

He waved the gun at her. "Careful. We decided you're only going to be flying me to Calgary tonight. March is going to stay here with Mrs. Er~ excuse me, Miss Parrish. Just to make sure she doesn't do anything stupid while she's waiting to hear from you. Wouldn't want Sergeant Elver calling his buddies in Calgary to have them snatch us up as soon as we land."

Garza looked at Parrish, whose face was stony and expressionless. "Are you okay with me leaving you alone with this guy?"

"I can handle him," Parrish said, gesturing with her gun.

"Okay, well. I need to get the plane ready. Fuel it up, move some things around..."

Loomis said, "Whoa, what do you mean move things around?"

"Weight distribution," she said. "Two of us on the plane, no luggage, the plane won't be balanced. I need to move some things around the cabin to make it more even."

"What things?"

She sighed and shrugged. "I don't know, man, emergency supplies, that sort of thing. It's just standard stuff."

Loomis still looked skeptical, but he waved her to the door. "Don't try anything funny. We'll be watching through this window."

"Get ready for a thrilling show." She looked back at Parrish one last time before she left the office. Parrish nodded once, and Garza took that as support.

She jogged across the tarmac. She remembered when she was younger, alone on a plane with Renee. They had fucked that afternoon, and Renee had worn a toy so she could... Anyway, that part wasn't important. The important thing was that on the flight back, Garza had suddenly gotten very sleepy. Extremely sleepy, out of the blue, so tired she couldn't keep her eyes open long enough to warn Renee she was about to fall asleep.

When she woke up, Renee was watching her from the plastic facemask connected to an oxygen tank. *"Unpressurized cabin,"* she'd said with a shit-eating grin. *"Took you up over twelve-five and it was lights out. Sorry. It's a bit of a hazing ritual. Don't be mad at me, please?"*

Garza climbed onto the plane and opened the emergency kit. Her supplemental oxygen tank was about the size of the fire extinguisher next to it. She took both and moved them to the forward part of the plane. Fire extinguisher behind the co-pilot seat, oxygen tank in front of hers.

"Don't ever do that with a passenger," Renee had warned her. *"It won't kill them, but it's dangerous and just a dick move in general. It's a mean prank. Don't do it."*

Garza had promised she wouldn't. But she had a feeling these were extenuating circumstances that Renee would have understood.

She went back to the emergency supplies and opened her kit for anything else she might be able to use. Cable ties, duct tape, scissors, blanket. She moved everything she thought might help to one of the biohazard bags and stowed it under her seat. Once she hit twelve thousand feet, she was going to have to move fast. She needed to breathe as much as Loomis did, and she was only ninety percent sure she could stay conscious long enough to get the mask on once he passed out. She had the benefit of knowing it was going to happen, to prepare for it, to feel its effects, know what they were, and fight against it. Definitely ninety percent certain.

Maybe eighty-five percent.

She decided not to think about percentages.

Once everything was situated where she wanted it, she went back to the office. She checked her watch and tried to cover her nerves with impatience.

"It'll be the middle of the night by the time we get there, so we might as well go now."

"Your girlfriend is in good hands." To March, he said, "Don't get in too much trouble without a chaperone looking over your shoulder."

Parrish was sitting behind Garza's desk, arms crossed. She rolled her eyes and shook her head.

Garza checked her watch again. "See you in about four hours."

"Be safe," Parrish said.

Loomis walked beside her as they left the office. "I got nothing against that, you know. Good-looking woman. And the red hair? Whooo, I thought she was a looker before! And you're kind of a mannish gal, no offense. It works for you. I'm just saying. I'm not one of those fire-and-brimstone fellas when it comes to what you girls are getting up to."

"So you're not one of those hardcore Christian murderers?"

He laughed. "Let he who is without sin, right?"

They got onboard the plane. She took her seat, while Loomis sat in the row behind her on the passenger side.

"We're pretty balanced, right?" he said, sounding sincerely concerned.

"Yeah, that'll work." She regretted that she couldn't see him without turning her head, but it was dark enough outside to make the windscreen act like a mirror. "Just try not to move around too much."

Loomis gestured with the gun. "I'll make the same request of you, sweetheart."

She grimaced and prepped for takeoff.

Once they were in the air, she said, "So this is really just about the money for you?"

"Not just this," Loomis said. "Life. Everything. It all comes down to cold hard cash. Money *can* buy happiness, little girl. Or at least it can buy you enough shit to distract you from being sad. Either way. You can't be truly happy if you're flat-ass broke."

"So you'd probably do anything to keep the money once you have it."

Loomis chuckled. "Starting to get a little worried?"

"I didn't say that," she said. "I'm just curious about how reasonable you're being. Considering the gun and breaking into my house in the middle of the night."

"Well, we just got lucky there, honestly. We didn't know Miss Parrish would be there. What a small world! And we needed you safe and sound to fly the plane. I don't know how to fly one of these things, and March doesn't even know how to drive a car. So we'd have been up shit creek without you. So this is what you'd call a mutually beneficial relationship. Once I'm in Calgary, I'll never think about you again. And once the bank transfer goes through, I'll be more than happy to erase Miss Parrish from my brain as well."

"Even though we'll both know where you went? And once you're gone, what's to stop us from going straight to Elver?"

He sighed. When he spoke again, his voice was lower, darker. "That would be a bad idea, actually. It would be best if we *all* forgot about tonight entirely. Don't you think?"

"Maybe so," she said

She glanced down at the altimeter. She nudged the plane higher, readying an excuse about better wind if Loomis noticed. It was hard to tell exactly how high they were even for her, given the dark expanse of empty fields below them. He might not even notice their altitude if he didn't have much experience in planes. She glanced over her shoulder. He was watching her, the gun resting on his thigh.

"Nervous?"

"Hard not to be with that thing pointed at me. Maybe you could put it away while we're in the air. It's not like I'm going to make a break for it. Besides, even if you don't mean to shoot me, accidents happen. We run into turbulence, you get thrown around a little bit. Gun falls out of your hand, it could put a hole in the side of the plane, and we'd both be screwed then."

He considered that. He apparently decided she had a point, because he leaned forward and put the gun in the pocket of the seat in front of him.

"Feel better?"

"Much."

"Just don't hit any turbulence."

"I'm adjusting to get out of the strong winds as we speak."

He nodded and looked out the window as if he could see the wind passing by.

The plane crossed twelve thousand feet. She kept climbing, despite the tingling in her fingers. She watched Loomis in the mirror on her console. His eyes drooped, and his head began rolling in slow circles as if he was listening to music only he could hear. Sometimes he slumped forward only to snap back upright with a grunt. His eyes drifted shut, but he remained upright in his seat.

"Long day," he said with a grunt, aggressively repositioning himself.

"You're not the one who got yanked out of bed in the middle of the night."

Garza felt like she was managing the effects of oxygen deprivation without too much effort. It was definitely harder to breathe, but she was in charge. She was in control. So she nudged it a little higher, ignoring the spacey feeling in her brain. She closed her eyes and then forced them open. Loomis' chin had dropped down to his chest and stayed there. She would give it a little longer. She didn't want to snap him awake and give him an adrenaline rush.

Finally, just when Garza was about to give in, his arms dropped limp out of his lap as if anchors had been tied to both wrists at the same time.

Garza grabbed the oxygen mask and slipped the elastic over her head, twisted the knob to turn it on, and took a deep gasp of the coldest, cleanest air she'd ever tasted. It was like a painless zap of lightning, immediately reviving her. She inhaled, exhaled, got her bearings back, and then she unfastened her seatbelt. The oxygen tank was portable enough that she could drag it with her while she did the next part, but that wasn't the most terrifying thing about the next few minutes.

She closed her eyes. She prepared herself. She checked the altimeter. Twelve-six-fifty.

Then she let go of the yoke and rose from her seat, letting the plane go into a freefall.

There was no autopilot, no way to let the instruments take over for a few minutes while she did what needed to be done. She just had to let it go and hope she had time to recover and straighten up.

With the tank in one hand, she grabbed the biohazard bag and moved to kneel next to Loomis. The first thing she did was use the cable ties to secure his wrists to the arms of the chair. The plane was falling. She pulled them tight, stopping just short of digging into the skin. He grunted and murmured, his bottom lip slack. The floor was sideways and gravity was pulling her toward the front of the plane, as if trying to urge her back to her seat. She pushed his jaw shut and put a strip of tape over his mouth.

The plane was falling.

Her heart pounded. She threw the blanket over his head, then tied it in place with a loop of duct tape around his forehead and jaw. It felt like she was literally falling out of a building. The plane couldn't be falling *that* fast, could it? She was sweating. She wrapped a loop of tape around his torso, pinning him to the chair. She had just torn off the tape when Loomis grunted, stiffened, and jerked at the cable ties around his wrists. He made a garbled noise behind his makeshift hood, obviously trying to work the tape off his mouth. She wrapped more tape around the outside of his hood just as an extra precaution.

Her stomach felt like it was somewhere near her knees as she retrieved his gun. Finally, gratefully, she got back into her seat. She grabbed the yoke and pulled up, bracing her feet against the floor as if she could physically get them back on course. She glanced at the altimeter and saw that they were at seven hundred feet.

Loomis shouted behind his gag.

"Sorry about that, sir," she said, "we had a bit of an emergency situation there, but rest assured I've got everything under control now."

Loomis threw himself forward, then slammed back against the seat. He rocked back and forth and, for a moment, Garza wondered if there was a real chance he might break it and get free.

"Mr. Loomis," she said, shouting over his animal protests. "I just risked blacking out and crashing us both into the prairie. And now I have a gun. Think about what I might be willing to do to shut you up and *fucking behave yourself.*"

He was breathing heavily, shoulders hunched, but he stopped trying to break the chair. Even in the reflection on the windscreen she could see that he was trembling with rage.

She focused on the world outside the window and brought them around. She couldn't go back to the airport. March would know something was wrong as soon as he saw her approaching so soon after leaving. She couldn't risk turning Parrish into a hostage. She considered her options, shook her head, and looked back at Loomis.

"Hang on tight, buddy. I'm about to do a second stupid thing in single trip."

She faced forward and shook her head.

"It's a new record..."

Sergeant Elver opened his eyes, looked at the illuminated alarm clock on his nightstand, and wondered who in their right mind would mow their lawn at half past two in the morning.

It took him another second to realize he wasn't hearing a lawnmower. The low, steady hum was growing louder, closer. He sat up and put his feet on the floor, trying to pinpoint a direction for the sound. Finally he got out of bed and went to the window, pushing back the curtain in time to see a small white and red plane pass by over the neighborhood. Its landing gear barely cleared the roof of his neighbor's house.

"Jesus *Christ!*" he said, ducking instinctively from the low plane.

His phone rang. He crouched to retrieve his pants and pulled them on as he hurried through the house. He yanked the receiver off the hanger as he buttoned them. His brain woke up enough to recognize where he'd seen the plane before, not that he'd seen a whole lot of planes lately. There was really only one person it could've been. He dialed Rais' number.

"That was Erika Garza," he said without waiting for her to say anything. She lived north of him and he knew she would've been woken up by the noise as well.

"I caught the numbers on the tail." Rais sounded energized. "Fucking thing nearly took off my chimney! What the *hell* is she thinking?"

"That's the first question I'm going to ask her," he said, hanging up on her as he went to get his uniform shirt from the closet.

Whatever her excuse, it had better be one hell of a story.

Chapter Sixteen

Garza had never thought about how wide city streets were. Her Cessna had a wingspan of about fourteen meters. Surely a two-lane street in Red Kite had to be at least that wide. How wide were cars? And there had to be space on either side of them. And a median, and sidewalks. She was fairly certain roads had to be at least fifteen meters wide. Anything less didn't make any sense.

That's what she told herself as she nose-dived toward Main Street. It was late enough that no one was parked in front of any businesses, thank God, but it still looked like it was going to be tight as hell.

Her heart hadn't slowed down since she restrained Loomis. Now she had to do something she'd done hundreds of times before - fly straight and land without swerving to either side - but with real consequences if she screwed up. She was sweating. She didn't know if she was blinking, but she doubted it. She just had to land. Easiest thing to do, Day One shit.

"Thread the needle," she whispered to herself.

She heard sirens and caught the shine of red and blue lights on the storefronts. A moment later, a cruiser sped out from underneath the plane. He continued on, clearing a path for her in case anyone happened to be out on the road at this hour. Thankfully he was smart enough to keep going instead of stopping at the intersection.

She hoped she was able to do the same.

The plane bounced as she touched down, jostling her but not too roughly. She'd had much worse landings. She didn't dare look to see if she was destroying the downtown storefronts, she just kept her eyes forward until the plane finally, mercifully came to a stop in front of the bank.

Sergeant Elver flipped a U and sped back toward the plane. Behind his cruiser, she saw another car speeding toward Main Street. Presumably that would be Constable Rais. Garza stood, her knees barely supporting her. Loomis was still breathing hard but was slumped forward with a defeated posture, fingers curled around the armrests.

"Did you hear those sirens, Loomis?" She patted his shoulder as she passed. "Your ride's here."

Elver was storming up to the plane when she opened the door. "Miss Garza, what in the *blue hell* are you *thinking?*"

She hooked her thumb over her shoulder. "The guy who murdered Saul is in there. I got him trussed him pretty well, I think. And I have a... I have..." She patted her pockets, checked the back waistband of her pants, and then looked back into the plane. "Shit. I *had* a gun... I took it off him. What the hell happened to it?"

"I'm sure we'll find it," Elver said. "Come down out of there."

Rais had parked and was walking up to them. Garza feigned a stumble as she stepped off the plane. Elver put a hand on her shoulder and she leaned into him to whisper.

"Christine is at the airport with another one. I had to leave her behind. I didn't have a choice. We've got to go back and get her."

"Okay. Let's get this settled first."

Garza wanted to demand immediate action, but she knew getting Loomis into a cell was the priority. Besides, as far as March knew, everything was going well. He wouldn't start to worry until they'd had enough time to reach Calgary. She looked at her watch. She still had a half hour before that happened.

She prayed it would be enough time and March wouldn't start getting anxious early.

Christine stayed behind the desk, watching the plane taxi down the runway and lift off into the night. March stood guard by the window, arms crossed, gun hanging in his pocket so heavily that it threatened to pull down his pants. She hoped he would sit down before that happened. Her own gun was sitting on the desk next to the phone.

She'd met both these idiots before. Doing her duty as Saul's good little wifey. They'd always creeped her out, talking about women like they were objects and money like it was a woman. March had always seemed to be a hanger-on, an expendable hanger-on that Loomis could get rid of if he became more trouble than he was worth.

She looked at the clock and mentally calculated how long it would be before they should expect Garza's call. She leaned forward and rested her hands on the desktop.

"Have you worked with that guy long?"

"Who, Loomis?" March walked to the client chair and sat down. "We started out together. The whole company was his idea. He's a genius. Made us rich. Made your hubby rich, too, until he got greedy. Stupid and greedy." He shook his head. "Some people, you know, they just don't know when to shut up and keep winning."

"Yeah. Or coming in second place."

March looked at her. "Hm?"

"Well, I mean..." She shrugged. "There's only one winner. So technically Loomis is the one winning, and you're coming in second place."

He narrowed his eyes and thought. "Well. I mean, sure, if you look at it that way. But we don't think of it like that. You know, winners and whatever."

"Sure. Yeah, I'm just talking. You're equals and you get paid the same." His face twitched. She raised an eyebrow. "You guys don't get paid the same?"

"He takes most of the risks," March said. "Being the boss, you know. There are expenses he has to... that he's responsible for."

Christine nodded. "Oh right! Yeah. Obviously. That makes a lot of sense." She leaned back in her chair. "Although. Well. With Saul dead and you two on the run, I don't know the details, but it sounds like your business is pretty much closed, right? So it would be smart to grab whatever you have and get to safety quick."

March worked his jaw from side to side. "You think he'd turn on me like that?"

"I don't even know the guy. I'm just watching from the outside. To me, I might think it's better to cut and run on my own instead of dragging around dead weight." She held up her hands to him. "No offense. Hypothetically. If I had a chance to get on a plane and ensure *my* escape, I don't know how much thought I'd spare for the guy I'm leaving behind." She smiled. "But maybe I'm just a heartless bitch. I'm sure Loomis is a stand-up guy."

March stood and paced around to the back of his chair. "You don't know him."

Christine shook her head. "I don't."

"He looks out for me. He doesn't have to give me anything, all right? I help him out and he gives me thirty percent right off the top."

"Thir–" She cut herself off, though she was sincerely surprised at how low the number was. "No, hey, if you're happy with that..."

"It's fair."

"According to you, or according to him? And thirty percent of what? The total he *claims* to have brought in? How trustworthy is that, if Saul was able to skim off you guys for so long without getting caught?"

He muttered a curse under his breath and went to the door. He stared out at the empty runway, still lit up by the security lights.

"He ain't coming back, is he?"

"Well, that wasn't the plan," she said. "The plan was for him to wait for you in Calgary. That's a long time for him to wait, though. Sitting in the airport for the whole time Erika flies back here, picks you up, and flies back. You know him better than I do."

March said, "He ain't waiting. Goddamn son of a bitch..."

Christine shook her head. "That's unbelievable. I'm sorry you got stuck with such a crummy partner." She swung the chair to one side, then the other. "Of course. If that's how he's going to treat *you*, then you might as well turn the tables, right?"

He looked over his shoulder at her. "What do you mean?"

"Well, he can't cut and run right now, can he? Up in the air, flying to Calgary. So you can screw him before he screws you. I can just give you my bank account information now and you can make a break for it."

"The, the cops..."

"They'll be looking for two guys, right? You and Loomis. You're just a businessman on a road trip. No reason to look at you twice."

He ran a hand over his face. "I-I don't know."

Christine stood up. "You could be the winner for once."

March tapped his foot on the floor. He was rubbing his hands together, having seemingly forgotten about the gun in his pocket.

"If Loomis caught me..."

"Loomis is hundreds of miles away, and he can't come back here looking for you. He'd be putting his own neck in a noose. He'd cut his losses and keep going wherever he was going in the first place. Hell, he probably won't even look back once they land. Leave you high and dry while he saves his own skin."

March shook his head and stepped toward the desk. "Fuck it. Give me the information."

She gestured at the phone. "I'll call the bank manager, my friend. I'll tell him the account is all yours, and he'll get the money together. Then you just have to go into town and pick it up."

He looked at the phone. Then at her. Then back at the phone. He chewed his lip. Finally, he nodded and motioned for her to make the call.

Christine picked up the phone and dialed. She remained standing as the ringtone chimed in her ear. "Good morning. At the tone, the time will be~"

"Hi, Scott. It's me. Christine." She grinned. "Christine *Parrish*."

"If you'd like to hear the current weather in your area, please enter your zip code~"

"I know! I know, I'm such a pain. But listen," she said, ignoring the automated woman. "This is very important. You know my account with you? Mm-hmm. That's the one! Well, I have a friend whose wife is having surgery. Oh I know. It's just awful. He can't afford it, and I can, and what good is the money doing just sitting there, right?" She laughed. "Right? I guess you *have* to buy me a drink the next time I'm in town. Oh, fresh! Okay. So, listen, he'll be there first thing in the morning to~"

March shook his head. "Have him transfer it to my account now."

"Um." She moved the receiver away from her mouth. "The bank isn't open now, Mr. March. Anything he does will have to wait until business hours. You'll have plenty of time to~"

"He's the manager! He can open the bank when he wants. Look..." He grabbed the receiver away from her before she had a chance to react. He pressed it to his ear. "Look, my name is Rob~" He frowned. Listened. Realization dawned in his eyes and he looked at Christine, his lips twisting into a sneer. "You bitch."

They moved at the same time. March was at a disadvantage, since he'd taken the phone with his dominant hand. He dropped the receiver and reached across his body with his weaker hand, trying to fish the gun from his pocket at an awkward angle. Christine grabbed the gun she'd left by the phone, also at a disadvantage because she'd never fired it before. She knew how, but Saul had never taken her to practice for real, so she had to hope the lessons had sunk in.

March's gun fired while it was still in his pocket, a loud pop followed by his scream, followed by Christine's scream, as she was certain he'd shot her. She reacted by pulling the trigger of her gun and falling backward, tripping over the chair, hitting the floor, and accidentally firing blindly as she hit the ground and her finger spasmed on the trigger.

She lay on the floor and stared at the ceiling. Gunpowder smelled like sharpness burning, and she wrinkled her nose. The only pain she felt was in her hip, where she'd hit the chair, and her head where she hit the floor. Her hip throbbed and her head felt like there was a nail in it. She risked a look down and didn't see any blood on her clothes. Her hands were shaking like mad, though, so she dropped the gun to avoid any further accidents.

The room was utterly silent.

"March?"

She heard something on the other side of the desk. Not a voice, not a sound a person should be making. But a response.

She rolled onto her stomach and crawled until she could peek around the side of the desk. She saw March on the floor, his hand outstretched and speckled with blood. The sound she'd heard was a man trying to breathe through a throat that wasn't entirely there anymore. She looked away and moved back so the horrific sight was blocked by the desk.

She closed her eyes and let herself shake, praying she hadn't just screwed Erika.

Elver slowed to a stop as soon as the airport was in sight. Rais had taken the passenger seat, so Garza was in the back. They had taken the time to take Loomis into custody, booking him at the station where a deputy was now standing guard. Garza had spent the entire process wishing they could speed things up, but now she wanted time to slow down, to delay whatever potential horrors might await them in the airport.

She leaned forward and scanned the office windows. The lights were on, but she didn't see anyone. She tried to ignore the block of cold in the center of her chest.

"They were in the office," she said. "There's no reason for them to go anywhere else in the house."

"Rest of the house looks dark," Rais pointed out.

"Yeah," Elver said, running his thumb across his bottom lip as he stared at the house. He unfastened his seatbelt. "Okay. You two sit tight."

He got out of the car, unholstered his weapon, and started toward the airport at a fast walk. He lowered into a crouch as he got closer, trying to stay below the window line. Garza wanted to jump out and run behind him, but she knew she'd only get in the way of anything he needed to do.

Rais drummed her hands on the car door, clearly antsy about being left behind. She made an impatient sound with her lips. Finally she looked at the rearview mirror and met Garza's eye.

"Have you landed a lot of planes in the middle of a town?"

"Nope," Garza said. "I was as surprised as you were that it worked out."

Rais twisted to look at her. "Any idea how you're going to get it off Main Street?"

Garza shook her head, eyes still locked on Elver. "I'll figure it out in the morning."

"Might want to wait until the paper has a chance to get a photo. They love it when something exciting actually happens."

Elver was almost to the airport. He sidestepped the square of light thrown by the window. He was so low that he was almost crab-walking when he reached the building. With his shoulder against the wall, he stretched his neck up and peeked inside.

Garza held her breath.

He stared hard at something, then raised up a little higher to search the rest of the room. He held his free hand up toward the car, palm-out, in the universal "wait" signal as he rose to his full height and went to the door. He entered the office and immediately crouched down to check something.

"Oh no," Garza whispered.

"Don't panic," Rais said. "We don't know what he's seeing."

Elver rose again and moved toward Garza's desk. He crouched down out of sight again, longer this time. Erika's hands were shaking. Her foot was bouncing enough that the entire car rocked from side to side, and she was grateful to Rais for not saying anything. Elver's head reappeared but he stayed down, crouched on the floor. He seemed to be talking to someone.

Garza muttered "Come on" under her breath.

Elver finally stood and bent down, arms extended.

He pulled Parrish to her feet, and though she slumped against him, she was moving under her own power.

Garza sagged forward and put her head down on the back of Rais's seat. "Oh God."

"Looks like your girl came out okay."

"She's not…"

Garza looked up and watched Elver and Parrish talking in the airport. She was sitting on the edge of the desk, and Elver seemed to be watching her face for signs of shock.

"Yeah," she said, smiling. "That's my girl."

Chapter Seventeen

Christine didn't know how long she was on the floor, staring at the ceiling, positive she'd been shot even though the pain from falling had faded and she didn't feel any evidence of a grievous wound. Eventually she heard the door open and went stiff, hoping for a savior, only relaxing when Sergeant Elver's face appeared above her. He looked concerned, then relieved.

"Miss Parrish," he said. "Burning the midnight oil?"

"Just taking a rest," she said. "How are you?"

"Doing just fine, ma'am."

He'd helped her to her feet and checked her eyes. "I think you're in shock."

"No, I haven't been shot," she said, slurring her words a little, keeping her eyes moving so they wouldn't be drawn to the dead man on the floor. "I'm just tired, is all. It's been a long day. Haven't gotten much sleep. Oh, Erika. She's in a plane. Somewhere."

The door opened and Erika came in.

"Oh, never mind, there she is. Where's your plane?"

Elver put an arm around her. "Okay, we're definitely taking her to St. Peter's to get checked out."

Rais had caught up with Erika. "Sorry, Sarge. She bolted out of the car."

"Don't worry about it too much, Sheila," Elver said. "I have a feeling even the fastest hound couldn't have stopped this rabbit." To Erika, he said, "You want to help me get her to the car?"

Erika slipped under Christine's other arm, taking her weight. Christine smiled at her.

"Hey."

"Hi."

"I don't think you went all the way to Claggery."

Erika looked past her at Elver, who explained, "Shock. Maybe a concussion from hitting her head on the floor. Sleep deprived. I don't think it's serious but..."

"Right," Erika agreed.

Christine opened her mouth as wide as she could, like she was trying to scream, then squeezed her eyes shut.

"This is crazy," she sang.

"It'll calm down soon," Erika said.

Christine nodded. "Good. Thank you, pretty."

She woke up later in the hospital, fully aware of the conversation. She'd thought she was making perfect sense and *they* were the weird ones. Mostly she recalled the long ride to the hospital. She remembered being in the backseat of Elver's cruiser with her legs in Erika's lap, head on her shoulder, being cradled like she was a baby. She'd very much enjoyed that. And she remembered watching out the window as they passed through town and hallucinating Erika's plane parked in the middle of Main Street. That had been quite surreal.

But now she was awake, and the events of that night felt like they'd happened weeks ago instead of just a few hours. Erika was sleeping in a chair next to the bed, her jacket draped over her chest like a blanket, feet up on the bottom edge of Christine's hospital bed. Christine watched her sleep, her own eyelids still very heavy and hard to keep up, but she didn't want to look away.

At some point she must have fallen back to sleep. Erika went from being fast asleep to sitting up scraping a plastic spoon along the inside curve of a pudding cup. She licked the pudding off, then noticed Christine was awake and watching her.

"Morning," Erika said. "I ate your pudding."

"How dare you," Christine said.

Erika glanced at the door, then stood up and bent over the bed to kiss Christine's lips. Christine sucked gently and got a small taste of the pudding left on Erika's tongue.

"Better than nothing, I guess," Christine said.

"I've had worse reviews," Erika admitted. She slipped her hand into Christine's. "How are you?"

"I think I'm better. I hit my head really hard, apparently."

"Among other things. The doctors took care of you, though."

"Hooray, doctors."

Erika smiled.

"So what happens now?"

"Well…" Erika sighed. "Elver told me what you did was a clear case of self-defense. I told him I'd testify that March was holding you hostage. There was a bullet hole in the desk, which means his weapon was also fired. So I don't think you have to worry about anything on that. And Loomis is talking, which is lucky. Constable Rais has been in with him since early this morning."

"So it's over?"

Erika shrugged. "Uh. I guess for us, it probably is. Loomis said the business was just him and March, and a couple of secretaries who didn't know what was really going on. And Saul, of course. With Loomis in jail and everyone else dead, I don't think we'll have to worry about anyone else coming after you."

"Good." Christine nodded. "Good." She looked out the window, then closed her eyes and let her head sink into the pillow. "What a night."

"God, it's only been one night." Erika sighed and shook her head.

Christine sighed. "I really don't know what I'm going to do now."

"That's okay," Erika said. "You don't have to decide right now. You can take as long as you need to. And if you need a place to stay, I've got room."

Christine looked at her. "Really? Still?"

Erika grinned and rubbed her thumb over Christine's knuckles. "What's changed? I know you a little better now. I'm a little more scared of you now."

Christine chuckled.

"I think we did this backwards. Most relationships end up being all about sex, all the time, and we started there without ever taking the time to... to... *meet* each other. I'd like it if we spent the next little while making up for that."

"I'd like that, too."

Erika held out her hand. "Erika Garza. Pilot, mechanic, delivery girl."

"Christine Parrish." She shook Erika's hand. "Unemployed and homeless."

"Maybe I can find some jobs you can do around my place in exchange for room and board."

"Jobs, huh?"

Erika said, "Yeah, I've got a few in mind. We can talk details when you're out of here and get back on your feet."

"Oh, so I'll be on my feet for these jobs...?"

"Maybe," Erika said, grinning. "Some of them. Sometimes."

Christine lifted Erika's hand so she could kiss her fingers. "I can't wait."

Garza wouldn't panic. She had put her life at risk to knock out a murderer, she wasn't going to be scared of Parrish.

But she was scared.

Rais had brought Parrish's car to the hospital, and Elver cleared them both to go back to the airport when she was discharged.

"Wait, we can just go back?" Garza said. "There... s-someone died there. You don't need to seal it off or something?"

Elver said, "I spoke with Anna Singh this morning. She confirmed it was clear-cut, so no one's going to have to worry about charges. I had a deputy working all night to get any evidence we might need, just to cover our bases, but there's no reason to keep you out of the place. He also cleaned up the, ah, the mess. If you were worried about walking in on that."

She hadn't even considered it. "Thank you. And, um, the next time you need... I don't know... an aerial search or something, just let me know."

"I'll keep that in mind, Miss Garza."

So now they were in the car. Garza was driving them, eyes fixed hard on the road, while Parrish sat in the passenger seat as quiet as she'd ever been. Garza had to imagine she was having a lot of the same thoughts and concerns.

They barely knew each other. And sure, they liked each other and had a lot of fun. In the bedroom. And at the baseball game. They were compatible in that arena without question. But now they were talking about actually *living* together. Sharing space in the house, day in and day out. That meant constant presence, dealing with Parrish as a human being taking up space rather than someone she liked and also had sex with, and there were any number of ways that could go wrong.

She had experienced many of those ways herself. The way she'd misread Renee. Other lovers who had come and gone in the interim, either too afraid or *far* too interested in commitment. People who she just could never see herself living with long-term.

Parrish seemed fine. Lovely. She would even go so far as to say wonderful. But that was how it always was at the 'let's move in together' stage.

The hard facts of the situation were that she barely knew Parrish in any real sense. If it didn't work out or~

"Thank you."

Garza looked over at her. "For... driving you home? I'm going that way anyway."

"No." Parrish smiled. Her eyes still looked so sleepy. "I mean for everything. Offering me a place to stay. For... a soft place to land, you know? Part of the reason I stayed with Saul for so long was because leaving him felt like closing my eyes and jumping out of a plane without checking to see if I had a parachute on. Now I have no choice. I should be terrified. But I'm just tired. But excited. To see what happens next. Thank you for being someone who makes me feel safe in a scary place."

Garza felt her anxiety fading. "Of course," she said. "You're welcome. I'm... I... It means a lot for you to say that."

When they arrived at the airport, Garza looked at the door to the office. "There's another entrance on the north side, if you'd rather~"

"Yes, please," Parrish said.

They walked around the building and entered through what Garza considered the side door. She was so used to coming in through the office that for a moment the house seemed backward. The living room was dark, with shafts of sunlight cutting around the curtain in thin gold bars. Parrish came in behind her and took her hand.

"So I guess I'll take the couch...?"

Garza smirked. "I mean, if you'd be comfortable there. I'm fine with sharing the bed. We can do a wall of pillows down the middle of the mattress to keep things clean."

Parrish laughed nervously. "I was joking. But. If you'd rather..."

"No." Garza stepped in front of her. "You're sleeping with me. It doesn't have to be sex, but I want you in my bed." She frowned when Parrish refused to meet her eye. "Did you think something had changed?"

"After last night?" Parrish said. "A-after I put you on a plane with an armed killer? And had people break into your house, and..." She hugged herself and shook her head. "I'm not sure *I* would want to sleep with anyone who brought all that shit down on my head."

"Oh honey." Garza pulled her close for a hug. "You didn't do any of that. And when guys showed up with guns, you showed up with your own and kept me safe. You're my hero, Christine Parrish. And if I have to knock out a hundred armed killers in order to be with you, then that's what I'll do. And I'll consider it a bargain. Maybe after I get a few under my belt, I'll figure out a way to do it without giving myself a headache."

Parrish reached up and petted Garza's temple. "You have a headache?"

"Yeah. A little one. It's better now."

"Poor thing." She leaned in and kissed Garza's forehead. "Do you want to go lay down and get some proper rest?"

"That would be great."

They went to the bedroom and undressed. Garza left her underwear on, but Parrish went fully nude. It was too hot for a full blanket so they just pulled the sheet up over them. Garza noticed that despite the fact Parrish was the taller of the two, she always ended up curled with her head on Garza's chest when they laid like this. She stroked her fingertips along Parrish's spine and listened to her breathe.

"Since you said those things about being scared," Garza said, "and that was probably hard for you, I should probably say some things that are hard for me."

Parrish looked up at her. "Like what?"

"Like... I'm really worried that we're moving too fast. We've only known each other two weeks. And yes, they've been two amazing weeks. I'm not questioning the times we're together. I'm just worried that we'll burn out and there won't be any fuel left when we're a month, six months, a year down the road. I'm scared of using us up."

Parrish pushed herself up, looming over Garza, nude and backlit by the window like a goddess. "I guess that's fair," she said. "But honestly, I've spent so long desperate to feel something like this, to be with someone like you, someone who legitimately cares about me. Someone who makes me feel safe and wanted and loved. Saul gave me what I thought I wanted. Money. A house. Security. He gave me what I thought was a life. But I was starving and didn't realize it. You showed up, and you're a whole meal, and the first two weeks have been making up for lost time."

She bent down and let her lips hover above Garza's.

"But now..."

She brushed her bottom lip over Garza's.

"...that everything is settled..."

She gave Garza the lightest, most fleeting kiss.

"...I'm going to savor every meal."

Garza licked her lips. Parrish was so close that the move let her lip Parrish's bottom lip.

"I know you said sharing a bed doesn't have to be sexual," Parrish said, her right hand already teasing the waistband of Garza's underwear. "But it *can* be... right...?"

"Are you hungry?" Garza asked, her breathing already rough.

Parrish slid down her body, pulling Garza's underwear down her legs as she repositioned herself on her stomach, feet lifted in the air as she kissed Garza's thighs.

"Starving."

Garza closed her eyes. She moved her legs apart and planted her feet on the mattress. When Parrish kissed her thighs, Garza realized there was something different about this time. It was a Tuesday, so it should have felt like they were back on schedule. Except... she looked at the clock. If it had been a normal Tuesday, she would've been in the air halfway to Calgary with Saul. She dropped her head onto the pillow and put her hand on top of Parrish's head. She threaded the still-unusual red hair through her fingers and pulled gently. Parrish lifted her head, lips wet.

"Does this feel weird to you?"

A line appeared between Parrish's eyebrows. "Weird bad?"

"No," Garza said quickly. "Just different than usual."

"Hm. Not really." She ran her tongue over her bottom lip and said, "Let me investigate further."

She put her head back down. Garza lifted her feet and placed them on Parrish's ass.

Halfway to her orgasm, she realized what it was. Why this time was unusual, what made the difference. This was a Tuesday without a Thursday, a real day with no ticking clock or endpoint. Christine Parrish was hers, for as long as she wanted her.

The realization made her breathe harder. She lifted her hips to Parrish's mouth and started whispering her name, making it into a chant.

No more ghost days, she thought as she came. Only real days from now on.

There was a kind of magic in that, too.

CHAPTER EIGHTEEN

"They're all going to hate me."

Garza laughed, then looked at Parrish and realized she was serious. "Why in the world would you think that? They don't even know you."

Parrish pulled her feet closer to the seat, which made her knees into peaks that she could rest her hands on. They were in Parrish's car, Garza driving because Parrish had said she was "too jumpy" to get behind the wheel. Garza was happy to drive but she was worried about whatever worries had pushed Parrish to the passenger seat.

Parrish finally shrugged in response to Garza's reassurances, eyes locked on the road. "I just know it. I can feel it."

"They're great," Garza assured her. "They'll love you. And, more importantly, you'll love them."

"We can just go back home," Parrish said. "I'll do that thing you like."

"I like all the things you do."

Parrish clarified, "The foot thing."

"Oh," Garza said. "I do enjoy the foot thing."

"Yeah, me too. So come on. Let's just go back."

Garza idled at a stop sign and looked at Parrish. "We can go home if you want. We can do the foot thing and fall asleep in each other's arms, and it would be a great night."

Parrish nodded. "I agree."

"But," Garza said, "that's not really living, right? It's not life. It's hiding. Cocooning. And there's nothing wrong with that for a little while. But eventually you've got to come out and see the world a little bit. Experience things. Meet people." She took Parrish's hand. "You really liked being with Saul at first. You were content with him, right? That's what you said? But then you just stayed in that house, you went from there to work, you read your romance books, and it got stale. I don't want to risk that happening with us. And people deserve to know you. You're pretty great."

Parrish took a deep breath and looked down at their hands. "I'm not going to know what to say."

"That sort of just happens," Garza said. "It's better if you don't have a script ahead of time. You just respond to people. It's called a conversation. It's fun, you'll like it."

"Fine," Parrish said with a resigned sigh. "But if I hate it, we never do this again. We just stay at the airport and only wear clothes when we absolutely have to."

Garza rolled away from the stop sign. "Sounds like a win-win for me, whatever happens."

Parrish smiled and bounced her foot, still nervous but clearly willing to go along with the plan. At least for right now.

"I'm serious, though," Garza said. "If you're uncomfortable at all, just let me know and I'll find an excuse to get you out of there."

"Thank you," Parrish said.

She relaxed then, and Garza thought she'd settled whatever nerves had been jangling in her mind. But when she parked at the curb, Parrish made no move to open her door. She just remained in her seat, staring at the house. She settled back against the seat and gave her time.

"Everyone in there," Parrish said slowly, carefully. "They're... they'll all be like..." She looked at Garza. "Like you?"

Garza raised an eyebrow. "Like me?"

"I mean." She laughed nervously and tucked her hair behind her ears.

"Gay?" Garza provided. "I think so, yeah. Is... that... a problem...?"

Parrish held up her hands. "Not for me! I'm just worried. I don't know." She breathed in deeply and let it out slowly. "I've never even kissed a woman before you. What if they think I'm faking or not really like them, like you?"

Garza chuckled and put her hand on the back of Parrish's neck. "*That's* what you're worried about? Sweetie." She leaned close and kissed Parrish's cheek. "There's a woman in there named Carol who was in her fifties before she accepted she was gay. Are you pretending when you're with me?"

"Being with you is the only time I'm not pretending," Parrish said.

"Then you'll fit in. And they'll love you. Like I love you."

Parrish leaned closer and Garza kissed her. "I love you, too, Erika."

"If you want to wait a little longer before we go in~"

"No. I'm ready now."

Garza nodded.

They walked up to the house together. Garza paused on the porch, put a hand in the small of Parrish's back to make sure she was still willing, then knocked.

Anna opened the door, smiling brightly, but her expression changed to confusion when she saw Parrish. She snapped her head to give Garza an accusatory look.

"You said *blonde*," Anna said. "Almost white!"

"Oh." Parrish touched her hair. "I-I dyed it..."

"It's a long story," Garza said. "And probably one that would be better told another time."

Anna nodded, waving her hands to dispel the first impression she'd just made. "Right. Right. I'm just very glad everything worked out for you both. You've been through a lot, Miss Parrish. How are you coping?"

"Uh," Parrish said, hunching her shoulders in a shrug. "It's not been the easiest thing in the world, obviously. It's hard to sleep some nights." She looked at Garza. "But it helps to have someone supporting me the whole way."

Anna smiled. "I'm sure. Well. Come on in! Most everyone is here already." She ushered them inside. Garza saw everyone but Amanda lingering by the kitchen doorway. Anna said, "Ladies, allow me to introduce you to the mysterious Christine Parrish, safe and sound."

Marie and Carol clapped. Carol came over and hugged Parrish, welcoming her home.

Anna said, "But tonight we're all just here to play poker. Erika, will you help Marie get the drinks and snacks and stuff?"

"Sure," Garza said, squeezing Parrish's arm before leaving her side.

Parrish looked at her, the anxiety gone from her features. She nodded, confirming she would be okay alone for a few minutes.

Once they were alone in the kitchen, Marie cleared her throat and spoke softly. "Be honest. How much did I miss by?"

"Miss...? Oh." She blushed and took the beers from the fridge. "Honestly, Marie, you're beautiful. And a lot of fun. And if we had met six months ago, who knows..."

She looked past Marie and saw Parrish in the living room. She was talking to Carol, eyes bright and animated, with a big sincere smile plastered on her face. She sensed Garza's eyes on her and looked up. She bit her lip and ticked her eyebrows a little, then turned her attention back to Carol. Garza remembered seeing Parrish for the first time, and then how seductive and undeniable she'd been that first night. Garza was lucky she'd been single when Parrish threw herself at her. But if she hadn't been... if she'd been dating Marie...

"It wouldn't have worked out," Garza finished. "And it probably would have ended very messy."

Marie looked over her shoulder, following Garza's eyes. She nodded knowingly.

"Dodged a bullet then."

"Yeah, guess so."

Marie grinned and thumped the side of her shoe against Garza's. "At least I took my shot. That's all we can do."

"Ain't that the truth."

Marie took the bottles. "I *am* planning to punish her by taking all her money tonight. I'm a beast when I'm playing for pettiness."

Garza laughed. "I think she can spare two or three bucks as retribution."

They carried the beer and chips back out to the dining room. Garza took her seat next to Parrish and squeezed her thigh under the table.

"Okay, all right," Anna said, shuffling the cards. "Plenty of time for life stories after the game gets going. Everyone ante up..."

***

Christine woke up and rolled onto her back, taking a few minutes to appreciate where she was. To appreciate *who* she was.

She was Christine Parrish. She was in the bed she shared with someone she loved, a person who loved her in return. The sun was shining through the window and she could hear the sound of breakfast being prepared elsewhere in the house. She rubbed her hands up and down her forearms in an attempt to calm the goosebumps there, rising just at the thought of how happy she was.

It had been two months since everything with Saul came crashing down. The terror of those first few days, even before she knew he was dead, sometimes felt like something that happened in another lifetime. She remembered the long run to Quebec, the panic that caused long blank stretches in her memory where she only surfaced long enough to make a decision before sliding back into oblivion again.

Coming back home had been the smartest thing she'd ever done. Even if it meant the night with Loomis and March, even if it had put her and Erika at risk. This was where she belonged. She was more certain of that than ever.

She put on Erika's robe and went out to be served her eggs and coffee. Erika was at the stove, already dressed for work, and glanced back when Christine said good morning.

"If you want me to pay you to just walk around looking like that, we can negotiate an hourly fee. You can stop trying to find a job in town."

Christine smiled as she settled at the table. "Thanks, but I think I'll try legitimate employment for a little while."

"Suit yourself," Erika said. "Sausage or bacon? Or both?"

"Is there enough for both?"

"Sure."

"Both, please."

Erika finished cooking and brought the plates to the table. "I'll be gone until after dark today. I have to fly some parts up to a factory in Fort McMurray. You can come with me, if you want."

"Is there anything to do up there?"

"Not really," Erika admitted. "We could spend the night in a hotel."

Christine raised an eyebrow. "As fun as that sounds, I think I'll stick around here and check a few more leads."

Erika said, "You know you could work here. Work the desk, take calls, schedule flights."

"I'll consider that a last case scenario. I'd love to work with you. But I feel like that would just be you paying me an allowance for doing chores around the house. I want a job. I want to earn a living that isn't connected to yours."

"I totally understand."

They chatted a while longer as they ate, then Erika had to prep for her flight. She wiped her lips, finished her milk, and stood up to kiss Christine goodbye.

"Won't take a ten hour flight with me, refuse to work with me... do you even *like* me, Christine?"

"You're not the worst roommate I've ever had."

"But not the best?"

Christine pretended to think. "Jury is still out."

Erika pouted and kissed Christine again. "I'll work harder."

"Well, do what you can. Are you going to stay the night up there?"

"Not if you're staying here. I'll be back in time for a late dinner."

"Fried chicken?"

"Sounds amazing. Thank you, love." She kissed Christine's hair. "See you tonight."

"Love you."

"I love you," Erika said as she grabbed her bag and headed out.

Christine poured herself another cup of coffee, then wandered outside. She watched the plane taxi down the runway, slowly gain speed, and then in a majestic lurch, rise up off the ground and start climbing. It didn't matter how many times she'd seen it, takeoff still took her breath away. She waved her arm over her head, then blew a kiss, unsure if Erika could see her or not. It didn't matter. It was their ritual, and she adored it.

She thought about the first time she'd come out to this airport. She wanted to say she had been a different person, but that wasn't entirely accurate. She hadn't been a person at all. She had been playing the part of Saul's partner, prim and proper and mysterious. And when Erika appeared, Christine thought she'd have to put on another character, become someone new to be with her. Someone bold and aggressive and seductive.

It had worked, it worked *very* well. Until feelings broke everything apart. Her whole world shattered even before she found out Saul was dead, and Erika Garza was the one who broke it. Just six days with her had been enough for Christine to realize no character, no mask, no playacting was going to be enough.

Erika had given her a chance to be herself. To feel, to want, to be wanted. That, as much as Loomis and March, had been what sent her running to Quebec. She'd spent so long faking life that the idea of living honestly scared the shit out of her as much as a pair of potential killers. But she came back because she realized how much she needed that. She needed Erika in her life, and the life that Erika could give her. It was a life worth fighting for, and Christine Parrish was someone she was desperate to be.

Her whole life had been nothing but ghost days.

She was ready to start living.

ABOUT THE AUTHOR

Geonn Cannon is the author of over sixty novels, including the *Riley Parra* series which was adapted into an Emmy-nominated webseries by Tello Films. His novel *Can You Hear Me* was adapted into Static Space, an award-winning short film. He's also written two tie-in novels for the television series *Stargate SG-1*. He was the first male author to win a Golden Crown Literary Society Award for his novel *Gemini*, and he won a second for *Dogs of War*.

www.ingramcontent.com/pod-product-compliance
Lightning Source LLC
Chambersburg PA
CBHW071937190726
48293CB00004B/1273